harmless

Julienne van Loon teaches creative writing at Curtin University in Perth, Western Australia. She is the author of two novels, *Road Story* (winner of *The Australian*/Vogel's Literary Award) and *Beneath the Bloodwood Tree*. Her short stories and personal essays have appeared in *The Monthly* and *Griffith Review*.

www.juliennevanloon.com.au

harmless

Julienne van Loon

FREMANTLE PRESS
fine independent publishing

For my father and mother

Adrianus Pieter and Jennifer van Loon

CHAPTER ONE
LOST

This sort of heat was too much for somebody his age. It was only nine in the morning, and already so ruthlessly bright. Back home in Thailand, the rainy season had only just finished and the moist air felt close and warm. This dry Australian air was different. He felt exposed by it.

Rattuwat turned back towards the bushland path they'd left half an hour before. At least there was some shade in that direction. It was unwise, actually, to have ever left the vehicle. But the child had convinced him that they were already very close to the prison and so he had begun walking for her sake. She was a child, after all, and she deserved to be able to see her father, especially after everything that had happened. Ah, Rattuwat, he thought to himself, you have been a fool to believe an eight year old's view of the world.

And now what? What could he do? The child had no respect. The child was impatient and rude. She did not understand that an old man like himself could not walk this sort of distance, especially in such heat. He took another step towards the shade of the trees, but paused to glance back over his shoulder at the girl. She was now just two twigs for legs sticking out beneath a faded red dress. She was a small girl in a big landscape. And was it wise, he wondered, to leave this girl on her own, to turn away from her out here in a place like this? What if she were your own daughter, he thought, and he remembered Sua at a similar age, so many decades ago, the way she would skip in circles around him in the family's electrical appliances shop in Ubon Ratchathani, her skirt flapping, her grin wide. Rattuwat touched his hand at his chest again. The burning pain was back. He stood motionless in the bare paddock. The sun beat down and he was overcome with grief. The little red dress walked on. 'She not know where to go,' he said, though nobody could hear him.

Amanda knew the way. The paddocks to their left, dry and pockmarked with salt, edged a thoroughbred horse stud she had driven past countless times with Ant. Nearby was a dry creek bed: Wooroloo Brook? They just needed to keep walking across these paddocks and soon they would come to the Great Eastern Highway again, where it curved to meet the roadhouse. The prison was further up the same road. It wouldn't take long. But then, maybe it would take all day, what with the old man trailing along at a snail's pace. She wished she could leave him somewhere, but knew also, that she would need him later on. They would not let someone her age into the visitors centre on her own.

She was worried. She was worried about what her dad had in mind for her.

Last year, before Sua had become ill, Amanda and her dad had visited the lake across the valley from here. They hired a canoe and rowed it right out to the middle of the tea-brown body of water. Amanda was being silly, singing 'I'm a Little Teapot' and tilting the canoe one way and the other. Her dad told her to settle down but she couldn't, and when she tried to stand up to do the gestures, the floor of the canoe slipped sideways beneath her feet. She remembered the earthy taste of the water, then the firm clench of her father's hand as he drew her upwards. When she resurfaced it was with a rush of air and light. The canoe was upside down, a narrow orange tent, and the paddles were floating off toward the reeds. Her dad was swimming in his clothes, laughing. 'You've got a big boogie coming out of your nose,' he said, pointing. And then they were both laughing. 'Oh, yuck!' and Amanda washed her face with her hand, dog-paddling.

Dad had been released to attend Sua's funeral on Wednesday. He was wearing civilian clothes and it was the first time in a long time that she'd seen him without the drab prison greens he wore every time she went to see him at Acacia. She thought he looked impossibly handsome in a long-sleeved collared shirt and the new black trousers Ant had chosen for him at the mall. They stood together in the front row at the funeral service, she a little in front of him so that his hands rested on her shoulders. Beside them was Ant, and on the other side, old Rattuwat. It was nice how Dad stroked her hair back from her forehead while the man at the front was talking, and it was this gesture, more than anything the celebrant said about Sua, that made Amanda cry.

'Listen, you have to book a visit,' her father had said to her later, when it was time to say goodbye. 'I need to see you and the old fella. Book a visit for the weekend. We need to talk about who's gonna look after you now. And besides, I might have a nice surprise for you.'

Stumbling down the firebreak, Amanda clenched her jaw. They were going to be late for the 9.45 booking. She felt a sudden lack of confidence, like a jab in the stomach. If only Ant had been home this morning, like he was supposed to be. If Ant had been driving, it would have been okay. The car wouldn't have broken down in the first place. Or else it would have broken down but her brother would have fixed it, right there at the roadside. Ant could be good like that. He knew how to do stuff. But Ant had gone out yesterday and not come back. Why did she have to get stuck with Rattuwat? The old man was useless. He'd stalled the car at almost every intersection. And half the time she could not understand what he was saying. She tried not to think about the sort of surprise her dad had in store. It couldn't possibly be a present, could it? Could they give presents to visitors? He never had before. Probably it was news. And she didn't want any more news. The only news that could make her happy would be to know her dad was coming home again. But he wouldn't be, would he? He couldn't be. Not yet.

Rattuwat could walk no further. He lifted his loose cotton trousers at the knee and squatted to rest. The bushland edging the firebreak was completely still, not a bird in sight. It was nothing like the moist evergreen forests back home. Here, it seemed there had been no rainy season at all. Flies clung to Rattuwat's back and flew periodically into his ears and nostrils. He looked down to lessen the effect of the sun's glare. Beneath his sandals was a bed of tiny but perfectly round pebbles, so easy to slip on. He ought to walk mindfully here, especially down the slope ahead. He ought to remember to do that.

The child wouldn't know what walking mindfully meant. She marched on; her limbs, though skinny, were strong and nimble, carrying her body easily along the gently sloping plain. The old man could see from the way she carried herself that she knew nothing of her own past. Part of him wished to be the one to tell her, another part – the wiser – thought it better to keep out of it, to keep his mouth shut. What kind of mother, he had speculated ever since the girl's older brother had told him the story, what kind of mother would do such a thing to her own child?

The girl stopped and turned back toward him, squinting. 'Come on!' she shouted. 'For God's sake, Grandpa. We haven't got all day.'

He was not her grandfather and he could not tell

whether she meant to be endearing or facetious in using that name with him. He stood up, keeping his legs bent and taking care to maintain a straight spine. The girl was waiting for him, hands on hips.

Rattuwat trod carefully across the shorn crop. It took him some time to reach her, and when he did, the girl took it upon herself to walk behind him, pushing the palm of her hand into the small of his back, marching him forward as if he were her prisoner.

'In my country, a girl not treat her grandfather this way,' he admonished her.

But the girl was impossible.

'Well, this is not your country,' she said.

And they walked on, the girl giving up on the pushing once she realised it did little to hasten the old man's progress.

Amanda's green turtle watch said 9.27 as she began to veer diagonally across the next paddock. There was no shade and she was without a hat.

The old man had fallen behind again. He walked oddly, she thought, bent forward and yet with such a carefully straight back. His knees pointed outwards. When she paused to wait she felt a little sorry for him. He was Sua's dad, after all, and if Sua were here now, she would want Amanda to treat him well. Amanda watched as the old man stopped to wipe his forehead with a rag.

She sighed. The thought that they would completely miss visiting time clouded her mind.

'Ananda!'

He could not even pronounce her name properly.

'Ananda!'

'An-an-da!' she mimicked, beneath her breath, exaggerating the old man's accent. 'An-an-da!'

'You not go right way,' he was shouting across the distance between them. 'You not know where you go.'

Amanda turned away, the singsong pattern of the old man's voice trailing away behind her.

'I not go with you,' he sang, his voice receding. 'You not know way. You think you know. You do not!'

CHAPTER TWO
NO SHOW

Something ached in Dave's gut as he waited on the bench outside the visitors centre. Amanda and the old man had three minutes left in which to show up. Dave had been jilted at scheduled visits too often, lately. Lashed, the cons called it, as if it hurt more than the old whip. Well, it did, in a way. He was always asking Ant to come with Amanda on a Saturday, but the kid managed once a fortnight, sometimes only once every three weeks. Half a dozen times already Dave had been looking forward to seeing the kids at their usual time, the visit booked and all, when the two of them had failed to show. The screws gave you half an hour before sending you back to your unit. He wouldn't have expected Sua's father to miss the appointment though. Christ, they really needed to talk things through, especially now that Maggie South was back in the picture. Would the old man be able to stay while they sorted the custody out?

Truth be known, Dave was a little bit nervous about

speaking to Sua's father. He wondered what sort of questions might come up. He wondered how much he knew.

Perhaps Dave could tell him about the very first time he saw Sua. He remembers it so clearly. He and the kids were standing around outside the Central Law Courts on Hay Street. It was Harley Trembath's court case, the one about the stabbing in the nightclub. Dave had more to do with it than the court would ever know.

'Come on, darlin',' he was saying to Amanda, still a toddler then. She had been screaming for nearly ten minutes. 'Don't do this to me now.' He was pressing his lips to the little girl's forehead, willing her to be quiet, blowing bubbles against her skin, trying to make her laugh. But she was turning her head, squealing, kicking her legs. Dave sometimes felt skinned alive by the girl's tantrums. The truth was he was still getting used to this whole parenting gig. Amanda's mother had dumped the girl on him and walked away when the child was barely a year old.

Ant was only twelve back then, shuffling relentlessly between Dave's place and his mother's. It must have been school holidays. Dave remembers watching his son tracing his finger along the shiny curve of an Alfa Romeo parked at the kerb. Then a black Mercedes pulled up.

'Ant, move.' The boy was in the way.

Dave shifted the sulking girl on his hip and watched the Mercedes driver get out to open the passenger door. That's when Harley's lawyer reappeared from between the rotund columns at the front of the building. Dave turned to face him. But the lawyer stopped still in his tracks, his eyes on the passenger getting out of the black Mercedes.

It was her: Sua.

She said nothing to either of them. There was a clean-shaven, respectable looking Steve Manning with her, his hand in hers, guiding her into the courthouse.

'Witness for the prosecution,' said Harley's lawyer.

Dave and the child both caught the scent of Sua's perfume in the air. She smelled like jasmine. Something larger than curiosity carried across the distance between them. Amanda stopped her whining. Sua turned back to look at them and Dave held her gaze for as long as he could. Then she was gone, along with her escort, into a sprawling, fluorescent-lit foyer.

'Steve Manning's squeeze,' the lawyer said, smirking at Dave. 'Import from Thailand. Not bad, eh? They sure do make 'em spicy over in Siam.'

It was just a glance given over a shoulder, but he remembered it. And when they met properly at one of Steve Manning's functions, months later, the connection had lost none of its heat.

Now the ginger-haired screw, Shiny they called him, ushered Dave up off the bench.

'You've had a no show, Loos. Sorry mate.'

'Oh, fuck this!'

He felt like kicking something. Shiny hovered a moment, towering a little. Dave looked down at his feet. He was not known as a troublemaker, or a whiner, or an arse. But Jesus, what a week. If they took away his visiting rights now, or threw him into DU, he feared he might not come out alive.

'You right, Loos?'

'Yeah, mate, yeah. I'm right.' Strained.

Back at M Unit, Dave went straight to his cell. He had nearly three hours to pass until Maggie South was due to visit. He'd hoped to get the girl all excited about Maggie. Talked her up. It might have helped, given him a bit of leverage. He could have told Maggie the kid was keen, then. Well, it wasn't to be. Dave's roommate, Lofty, was out watching the prison footy match; some of the guys in the can could play as good as old 'Such is Life' himself but hadn't been given half the opportunities. Lofty was right into it, following the M Unit footy tipping like some kind of born-again might follow the great Book. It was about all he could follow, poor bloke. Dave was grateful to have the room to himself for a bit. He switched the movie channel on, and sat down on the bed.

It would be something simple, he figured. Ant probably hadn't shown up to drive them. Then they'd have missed the bus. But the thought of the old Thai, dazed and confused with his minimal English, wandering about with Amanda in tow, didn't console him one bit.

'God, please,' he said to himself, 'let them be safe.'

It was now twenty years, almost to the day, since Dave's first adult conviction. He remembered how his mother, bless her, had sat outside the district courtroom all the way through that first case. She waited for morning tea, lunch, every small adjournment, for news from the legal counsel provided free-of-charge by Legal Aid. She refused to step inside the courtroom. What was she frightened of? The lawyer told him she passed the time reading a book. What book? Dave wondered now, two decades later.

Back then, Dave had been charged for an offence he was alleged to have committed ten days after his eighteenth birthday. A fortnight earlier and he would have been charged in the children's court. It was his first experience of being stripped down to the bone in front of a judge and jury. By the time the two-day trial had finished there was little about him that those present in the courtroom did not know. They had something of every part of his life's narrative thus far: his family history, his employment history, the various relationships he'd had with women, the names and occupations of his friends. They knew about his history as a drug user, they knew he'd started seeing a psych at the age of twelve (a court order at the time). And they'd been led through his every movement in the twenty-four hours leading up to the moment-of-interest. Dave sat on the bench reserved for the accused, directly facing the jury, and within easy grasp of the court security guard who had been employed to watch over him. He glanced across at the jurors when he felt nobody was looking. There was an arrogance about them. It was as if they had condemned him, even before the first day's sitting was through.

He still remembered travelling from the holding cells beneath the courthouse through to Canning Vale that first time in the back of the prison transport vehicle. He spent the whole time looking out the heavily tinted window. Everything on the outside had a blue-black tinge to it, and the people of Perth were going about their everyday lives as he went by, lighting their cigarettes, sipping at their coffees, pushing their children in strollers. Dave looked out at them. He felt as if he were travelling in a parallel universe. In some ways, all these years later, he still hadn't left it.

The thing was, all through that first night in prison, it was his mother he was thinking of. How she'd be faring in her new retirement unit in Scarborough. Making her tea in a pot, the old-fashioned way. Sitting down to the news in front of the box. Brushing her teeth, climbing into bed in her blue and white floral nightie. He thought about how he'd disappointed her. Flatly, fully, permanently.

She was not there the next time he went to court.

When Sua first came into Dave's life, four years ago, he'd had the two kids on his own for a time, and a part-time day job at Harvey Norman in Midland, selling computing. But that was only for the taxman. His other work was with John Hart, moonlighting. This was 2006, the year they did the king of all heists down at the university in Bentley. They shifted nearly a hundred and fifty units in one night. Not a whisper. Totally smooth.

He and John got cocky after that. They had this plan that if they did three or four other campuses the same way, all in the same week, people would figure it was an out-of-town job. Hit and run. It worked, too. Within ten days they had a warehouse full of state-of-the-art technology. They had a container ship lined up. It was perfect, all of it. It would set them both up for years. They should have just stopped at that, hey. But John wanted a little extra. On the last day of the week, they took out a whole lab's worth of computers in broad daylight from the TAFE college in Leederville. They had uniforms on and a van with a fake logo on the side.

People like to think of Perth as a big city now. But behind the glassy skyscrapers in the CBD, behind the glittering night lights bouncing off the surface of the river, there remains a pretty small network, really, a pretty small town. People know each other. John knew Steve Manning. And Manning had a bit of extra storage space. Hush hush.

Humphrey Bogart was on the television screen again. These stilted old American flicks from the forties and fifties, there was an art to them, sure, but it was all so severely stylised, as if things could only be played one way. How many more decades would he need to endure them? These were the sort of flicks that Maggie South loved. It was a world so perfectly rehearsed.

He glanced at the corner of his mattress, beneath which was the letter Maggie had sent in reply to his own of a week ago. 'It's not a good time,' she wrote. 'I've barely put my own pieces back together. I've been straight for nearly a year. I've finally gone back to school, and my teacher at the TAFE (half my age!) says I should write a book about everything that's happened. Stranger than fiction, she reckons. And that's what I want to do, Dave, write it all down. But it's not easy. It's all I can do just to stay clean right now, and I can't guarantee that payday, every single fortnight, won't be the death of me again.'

And yet she was coming. She was coming at one o'clock. There must have been some part of her that was still thinking about taking Amanda back. Who else was there now? It would either be Maggie or the State.

Dave's arse was numb. He'd always hated having to sit still.

In jail, the real trick was to try and keep busy. It was the waiting around that killed you; sitting there too much, thinking too much, getting too caught up in your own head. The justice system had continued its gradual and relentless expansion of the prison population in the months since Dave had been in custody. They'd already moved bunk beds into all the cells in J and K Units; he'd heard M Unit would be next. The place was built to house seven hundred; there were nearly a thousand here now. And it was happening all over the State. Up north in the regional prisons they'd thrown three men into cells meant for one. Some poor bugger sleeping with his head up against the toilet bowl. What do they do about matchmaking, those bastards that run the State prison system? Do they run a check to see whether the three of you have a few things in common before they throw you together in a cell the size of an ensuite? He had been lucky with Lofty; he was a violent offender, but as it turned out he was on Zoloft most of the time. Everything Lofty did was sugar-coated, blurry. The world slowed down for him. Dave hated the idea. Time in the can went slow enough already.

Eleven o'clock. Nothing about the day had changed. The sky was still the same blue: light, infinite, clear. Fang, an old con with too many teeth missing, sat beside Dave on the bench outside their unit and shared a smoke. The old con sat with his knees wide apart, a rollie in one hand. In his own way, Dave supposed, Fang was trying to console him.

'Heard of a fella who escaped Hakea once,' Fang reckoned, 'and got away with it, too. They never did find him. He moved up the Kimberley, lived out the rest of his days up there, eh.'

The old con's network was full of gossip, and if even half of it were true, there had been some pretty amazing feats on the part of cons that had never made it to the papers.

'This fella was in prison for life, maximum-security too,' Fang went on. 'Never did skite about how he got himself out. No one knew. Must have been some kind of genius, they reckon. The thing is, afterwards, he set himself up on a property up in the north-west, middle of bloody nowhere. Didn't like to receive visitors, eh.

'A bloke I knew made the trip up there to see him. He'd rigged up all this high-tech security, all around the perimeter fence. This is out in Western Desert country, dunno if you know it, flat as a pancake, dry as a nun's cunt. What the bloody hell would you do out there? Fuck knows.

'Anyway, you know what happened?'

Dave raised half an eyebrow, but before he had time to guess, Fang kept talking.

'I'll tell you what happened. He went mad, completely fuckin' mad. Fearful of every little tick, every little spark. Me mate Old Johnno went up there, eh, saw it for himself. He'd known the fella for decades, been through all sorts of shit together, inside and out, you know? He gets there and the fella wants to check out the boot of Old Johnno's car, right? So, he shows him the boot, nothing in there but a litre of oil and a bit of coolant for the radiator, mate, a few barrels of water and that. Next thing you know the old bloke is trying to give him a knock on the head, seriously, his best mate, he'd got that bloody paranoid. Old Johnno talks him through, you know, calms the fella down. But then there's a breath of wind, clanging on an old bit of iron, bang, slap, enough to fill him with absolute bloody terror. He's rushing around, back and forth, checking out this and that. It was like he was still in jail, mate. Except in the can he wasn't shitting himself every waking minute. In the can, people had respect for him, you know what I'm saying?

'That's it, you know, that's how it is. I listen to all youse young fellas, youse think ah, it'd be easy. Every one's got some nutty plan for a jailbreak. What then, but? What about after? You can't escape the fear, mate.

Go anywhere in the world if you want to, but you can't escape the fear. It eats you up from the inside out. Fucks you up in here,' he said, tapping his head, 'you know what I'm saying, buddy? Fucks you up in here, worse than the can itself, mate, fuckin' heaps worse.'

CHAPTER THREE
PULLING ORCHIDS

Amanda's legs were beginning to ache and her elastic had come loose, spilling hair into her eyes. Her green turtle watch said 11.23 as she flopped herself down in the shade of a big jarrah. She knew now that she was never going to make it to the prison, and she felt bad about leaving old Rattuwat behind. Looking back along the track she had followed down the edge of one paddock and diagonally across the next, she could see no trace of him. She tried to remember which bushy outcrop it was that she had left him at, but they were all beginning to look the same. He might have been right, anyway. She had to admit now that she was not completely sure about the path she had chosen. She knew that they had needed to head away from the city when they left the car, but the car was long out of sight, as was the highway, and now she wasn't sure which way was which.

Someone once told her that you could tell the direction from the sun just by looking at it, but she had looked at the sun, high above, and it was giving away nothing. Besides, she couldn't quite understand what it meant to read direction from the sun. It was so far away. How could it lead everyone at the same time?

Amanda kicked off her shoes. Her feet were hot and sore. She nursed one foot in her lap, massaging her sole like Sua used to do sometimes. Sua knew how to do a foot massage properly, with strong warm hands and firm fingers. It always made you feel relaxed. Amanda didn't have Sua's strength and she was not sure about where you were supposed to press. Her fringe fell in her eyes again.

She wiped clear the lens of her turtle watch. Late last year, she and her friend Laura had taken to mucking around on the Habitat Heroes website in the school library at lunchtime. All the avatars were endangered species. Laura was a black and white panda. Amanda was a green turtle. She loved to imagine herself beneath the sea, where her huge turtle mouth was always gently smiling. Also, turtles grew old, really old, sometimes a hundred years old. She felt old too, sometimes, sort of wise to things not everyone could see. Green turtles live in the Gulf of Mexico, and when Amanda chose them for her avatar there were only a few hundred of them left in the wild. Then, three weeks into April, there was the Deepwater Horizon oil spill. They saw pictures on *Behind the News*. Pelicans bathed in oil. Big blue-grey plumes of poison floating on top of the ocean. Whenever the pictures of the spill showed up on the TV news at home, Amanda looked away. But she carried the images with her anyway, like murky photographs. Somehow over the weeks, she'd come to think of her real-life self as being, in part, green turtle, and of the real green turtles swimming around in the Gulf of Mexico as being, at least in part, herself. The thing about the oil spill was that nobody could fix it, not even the president of America. It was a bit the same at home. When she came home from school not long after the Easter break to find Sua collapsed in the hallway, a bloodied bruise forming on her forehead, she knew it was the beginning of something terrible. And without her dad around, nothing could be fixed.

Sometimes, when she visited him in jail, her dad told her stories of when he was a kid. Catching tadpoles down at the creek and trading them at school for other kids' home-packed lunch. Hiding under the cattle grid at the front gate when the school bus stopped to pick him up. Setting up obstacle courses in the backyard, and running a betting ring with the local kids as to who would complete it in best time. There was a lightness about him when he told her these stories. She wanted him to repeat them, again, again.

A little in front of the old jarrah where Amanda now sat, there was a small collection of blue lady orchids, sheltering near a granite boulder. Her dad loved those. The petals were a delicate sky-blue. He told her once how orchids like these loved to open in the sun. They went all shy on cloudy days. Sometimes in the early spring she and her dad would go looking for orchids together in the reserve behind their house. The colours seemed more intense closer to home. The group before her now bore a lighter, almost powdery-blue petal. It was rare to see them flowering so late in the season. Amanda shifted from her seat to take a closer look. There were four altogether. Just like her family: Dad, Sua, Ant, Amanda. Except Sua was gone now.

It was almost a whole year now since all four of them had been at home together. Amanda remembered one of those rare days, last winter holidays, when rain was falling hard and the house was closed up and the dreamy rhythm of raindrops, beating, dripping, spilling down the pipes outside, was a source of comfort. In the background, she could hear Dad and Ant using power tools in the shed. They were trying to fix Ant's car. On the kitchen floor, Amanda had set up all three mismatched sets of dominoes, standing the tiles upright in swirls and patterns all along the lino. She had made the shape of the letter S for Sua.

'See if you can blow the first one down,' she said to Sua, demonstrating with a pout of her lips. Amanda remembered how Sua squatted beside her to blow, and then the delicate percussion as the tiles fell, the precise poetry of small-scale destruction as they splayed.

'It's not fair. Your letter is better than mine,' she told Sua. It was impossible to set the letter A in motion in the same way.

'Life is not fair,' Sua laughed.

'I know.'

They began to design more complex systems, requiring

the tiles to fall from table to chair, then from chair to floor. Would the connections work? Would the trigger tiles land predictably enough from one level to the next? It was a game of patience, so easy to knock one section accidentally, and have to set up all over again. Amanda watched the concentration on Sua's face, the way a swatch of her hair fell diagonally across a cheek. Her face was brown and smooth and flawless. Her fingers were fine.

'What was your mother like?' she asked her.

Sua smiled. 'She's still alive. She lives in Thailand.'

'Do you miss her?'

'Yes.'

'What is she like?'

'She has a happy heart. Generous. At home in Isaan she always looks after people. She works hard.'

'I miss my mother, too, sometimes.'

'Okay.'

'I don't remember her, but I still miss her. Do you think it's silly, to miss someone you don't even know?'

'No.'

They were ready to trigger the latest experiment.

'You blow,' said Sua.

Amanda blew too softly at first. And then again, harder. It was by some miracle that the course worked flawlessly, straight through. Every tile fell perfectly into place. Amanda held her breath as she watched.

'Let's do it again and show the boys,' she said, when it was done, and together they put all the pieces back in place. 'My mother couldn't love me,' she told Sua. It was a belief she had never been able to voice with her father.

'I love you,' Sua said.

The girl smiled. 'Yes,' she said, as Dad and Ant appeared at the kitchen door. 'I know.'

Amanda planned to have heaps of kids when she grew up. She thought maybe six would be about right. Some of the kids at school came from big families. Once she went to Riley Foreman's house for the weekend, because his dad was a friend of her dad, and they were working on some project on the computer. The place was a constant whirl of noise and laughter. There were ball games and pillow fights. There were three kids to a bedroom. You never lacked for someone to play with at their place. Mrs Foreman was forever at the kitchen bench buttering toast, or at the washing line handling clothes. She bellowed out orders which nobody seemed to follow. There were eight Foreman kids, and Amanda had heard a rumour just lately that the eldest girl, Freya, was pregnant already, at sixteen. Amanda didn't want to be like Freya, or like Mrs Foreman, exactly, but she knew she wanted to make some kids a home. She'd be good at it. She would be sure not to mess it up.

When she grew up, she was going to be All Organised, like Laura's mum, only not so sharp in the way she spoke to people. She was going to be honest, and trusting, like Sua, the best kind of friend to her kids, the kind of mum you could tell anything to. And she was going to be happy, like the mum in *Gilmore Girls,* always smiling. Sometimes she tried to picture her own mother's face. She had no photographs. Dad told her once that her mother was 'a bit of a hippie' and so she imagined a long-haired woman with loopy earrings and long skirts, perhaps a scarf on her head, but maybe she was confusing *hippie* with *gypsy*. She wasn't entirely sure of the difference between the two.

'When I was a girl, I always wanted children,' Sua confided once on the way back from the supermarket.

'Can't you have them?'

'When I was a young woman, I had problems. The doctor told me no.'

'Oh, that's not fair.'

It seemed families were sometimes given to the wrong people.

Amanda tried to imagine Sua as a teenager. Did she finish high school? When did she first have a boyfriend? What was he like? For all the talking they'd done, Amanda knew nothing of these things.

Right now, the little group of orchids before her seemed parched in the heat. She touched the tallest with an outstretched finger. Was this one the mother orchid? If this little group were her family, the tallest one would be Dad, she thought. And the next tallest would be Ant. And the short ones, Sua and me. What about her real mother? She gripped the tallest orchid at its base with thumb and forefinger and tugged a little. In all the time she had admired orchids, she'd never been allowed to pick them. And she wasn't about to do so now. But then it occurred to her that maybe she could carefully uproot one – just for a minute – so as to see the whole length of it. She could call it an experiment. She gripped the frail stem firmly and the single taproot came out easily. It was almost as fine as a strand of her own hair. As she lay the plant down on the ground, she wondered if it really was the tallest. If you were to work out the length from the bottom of the root all the way up to the top of the flower, it might not turn out to be the tallest after all. She took the second one out, the one that might have been Ant. Actually, its roots were a little bit longer than the daddy one. Perhaps it was the eldest. Soon she had all four plants laid out in front of her. If it were her job to deliver water rations to each of them, she would give the tallest one the most. He was the old man, Rattuwat. Daddy would get the next biggest drink, and she and Ant would share what was left. (Sua didn't need an orchid. She was gone now.)

It was only when Amanda tried to put the first of the plants back into its place in the ground that she realised what had happened. She couldn't thread the root back into its hole. It wouldn't go. The slender stem wouldn't stand up on its own anymore. She drilled her finger into the ground to widen and deepen the hole but it was no good. It still wouldn't go back in properly. It drooped. They all did.

Amanda wanted to get it right. She didn't want to be blamed for what had happened. It was not her fault, surely. It was not what she intended.

'I've killed them.' She looked back across the course she had followed through open farmland but the old man wasn't coming and she felt certain she'd missed something special at the jail. Maybe her dad *was* coming home. She felt bad. The paddocks across the way were dreadfully empty. It seemed the old man, Rattuwat, was lost and if something bad had happened to him that, too, was probably her fault.

CHAPTER FOUR
LETTERS AND SYLLABLES

Rattuwat crossed his legs, rested his hands in his lap and shut his eyes. He had never before been so far from home. It was exhausting. He needed to sit completely still, to recharge. He had learned to meditate as a child, and although he spent many decades as an adult neglecting the art, in recent times it had given him solace. In the still afternoon air, he breathed in, and felt the unrelenting hardness of rock beneath his buttocks. He swallowed, sank into the black emptiness behind his eyes, breathed. He would dwell here in the quiet dark, conscious only of the rise and fall and rise and fall of every inhalation, exhalation. His mind turned inward, the silence like a second home. He was withdrawing from the world of the girl in the red dress. He was no longer in her country.

In the letters she'd sent him every month since leaving for Australia, Rattuwat's daughter had described her husband as a good man. He worked at an iron ore mine, she wrote, and his company flew him north to the remote site for eight days every fortnight, then he spent five nights at home, a kind of long weekend. Sua described their home as a large house with four bedrooms and a small courtyard garden in which she grew orchids in hanging pots. She described her time as a student, first at an English language college, and later at a hospitality school, where she learnt to manage hotels.

In mid-2005 she sent news of a pregnancy, and early the next year a photograph of a newborn girl. She told her parents the girl's name was Chloe and that she and the Australian had taken the child to a forest monastery on the outskirts of Perth, where the head monk, an Englishman who had trained in the Thai tradition, gave the newborn girl a traditional blessing.

Photographs of the grandchild came only occasionally after that. Before the first child was eighteen months old, she was joined by a sibling, a boy. Rattuwat felt that this was right; in their family the children always came in the same pattern, girl then boy then girl then boy. Other families had envied the Suhikarans their even reproductive fate. Their houses had plenty of girls to help with domestic labour; and enough boys to spare at least one son to the monastery, although in the case of his own marriage, something went wrong. Thawin never again fell pregnant after their twins were born.

At home in Bangkok, in the dark before dawn, and again before retiring at night, Rattuwat and his wife knelt before the shrine in their room above the flow of Khlong Saen Saep, and chanted the blessings. They had spent the last few years sharing the merits of their offerings with the two farang grandchildren they had not yet met. The girl, Chloe, the boy, Michael. The babies' photographs were placed respectfully beneath the photographs of three elderly monks – kruba ajahns – who still resided in monasteries at home in the north-east.

When he was met off the plane in Perth earlier in the week, Rattuwat expected the two little ones to be there to greet him. But the Australian had sent an older boy, a boy he'd never heard of: Ant.

Ant reminded Rattuwat of his son Arthit at a similar age. There was a sly confidence about him. The car that awaited Rattuwat in the airport carpark was sleek and black, its windows heavily tinted. Two fluffy dice hung from the rear-view mirror in the place where a Bangkok driver would have arranged a whole string of Buddha rupas. Boom-boom music roared from the stereo when the ignition was switched on. At least the boy had respect enough to switch it off as the old man got in.

As they reversed out of the parking space, Rattuwat was surprised by a movement in the back. He turned to discover a small girl sitting there. She was perhaps seven or eight years old. She smiled wanly back at him and something about her wide blue eyes was powerful, unsettling.

'Hello,' he said to her. 'Who are you?'

'Amanda,' she replied, as if that would explain things.

At first, Rattuwat thought that these two children might be the cousins of his own grandchildren. He would ask his son-in-law, later, for the details.

'Good you drive me, very kind,' he said to the boy, who mumbled something unrecognisable in acknowledgement.

Perhaps the Australian had been married before. If so, Sua had never mentioned it.

Their car travelled smoothly along the sort of wide, clean roads Rattuwat remembered from his daughter's descriptions of the new city, and they soon formed part of a neat trickle of traffic, all shiny, well-kept vehicles, no tuktuks, no motorbikes, barely a single pedestrian along the road's edge. Nobody sounded a single horn. It was indeed a tidy, bright and well-organised place, just like in the pictures he had seen on occasional postcards.

The three travelled mostly in silence. Ant took them along a winding road that rose into the ranges to the east of the city. Suburban shopfronts gave way to bushland, interspersed with small citrus orchards and occasional dry paddocks. They passed several interstate trucks making slow progress up the incline, and the boy overtook these with the self-assurance of a young driver who has not yet been involved in an accident.

After almost an hour they turned off the highway and followed a narrow tree-lined side road into and through a small village. Even here, the streets were empty of pedestrians. One of his friends at home had warned

Rattuwat about this: apparently everybody shopped and ate indoors in Australia. The streets and gardens were almost always empty. Something about this fact unsettled him.

Before long, the vehicle was slowing again as the boy negotiated the turn into a driveway partly hidden by shrubbery. They crossed a dry creek bed and pulled into a new steel garage that dwarfed the single-storey cottage nearby. The house was in poor condition. The guttering, full of rusty holes, swung from its anchoring. The glass in one of the windows was broken. At the kitchen door they were greeted by a small grey dog whose head trembled and shook like an old woman. Rattuwat was disappointed to discover that there was nobody else there to greet them.

'Dad's still in the can,' Ant told him. 'He said to tell you he'd see you at the funeral tomorrow.'

The children were ill-mannered hosts. The boy's mobile phone buzzed and beeped for most of the afternoon. There was the air of an entrepreneur about him: he seemed to be brokering deals. The girl curled up with the nervous dog in front of a large television in the largest room and seemed unable, or unwilling, to take any interest in making Rattuwat comfortable. He found his own way to a bedroom overlooking an unkempt little orchard. He placed his small suitcase in an empty corner. When he caught his reflection in the mirror on the wardrobe door he noticed a photograph wedged between the mirror and its frame. It was Sua.

Her joyful smile was a comfort to him. So, he had come to the right place after all. He plucked her picture from the frame's fragile hold and studied the face of the man who stood beside her. This was not the same Australian Rattuwat had given his daughter permission to marry so many years ago. And yet he knew with a cold certainty that this was the man he had spoken to on the telephone last week. In the photograph, the man's face was warm and open, host to a broad smile. He was without a shirt; she was wearing a bikini. They seemed happy. Rattuwat wanted to keep the photograph, to take it home to his wife. He opened his suitcase to place the picture inside, but paused. It was not rightly his to take. He placed it tentatively back where it belonged and decided to follow his wife's instructions, that is, to hang up the carefully pressed clothes he was to wear to the funeral. He set aside the little gifts Thawin had sent for the grandchildren and retrieved the black, Western-style suit trousers and collared shirt the local tailor had made for him only days earlier. He hung it on the door of the cupboard. It would need a light press in the morning. Perhaps the girl would do it.

Despite his intentions, Rattuwat could not take his eyes off the photograph of Sua. He took it down once more, held it in both hands, and bowed his head for a few moments. Then he took the picture, along with another carefully wrapped package from his suitcase, and went to find the girl. She was still sitting with her feet tucked beneath her on the lounge chair, running her fingers through the dog's coat.

'Your father, yes?' he said to her, holding up the picture.

'Yes,' she said, and for the first time she gave him a genuine smile.

'Ah,' nodded Rattuwat. 'He a happy man.'

The girl beamed back at him.

'Ant took that picture,' she said proudly. 'We went to the beach at Scarborough. It was Christmas, just after Sua first came to stay with us. I'm in the picture too, you know,' she said. 'Look how short I am,' and she pointed to a curve of beach towel crowning a head of blonde hair, barely visible in the bottom corner of the frame. 'I was only four.'

'Please,' said Rattuwat, offering her the package from his suitcase, 'for you. My wife send some Thai sweets. We call this *look chup*,' and he watched the girl's eyes widen as she spied the little sweets in bright reds and greens, perfectly moulded into the form of miniature fruit. 'Sua love *look chup* when she small,' he told her.

They smiled at each other, the smaller one popping the first of many sweets into her mouth. In this way, they made it through the afternoon.

The next morning they made the journey to the funeral parlour, retracing their path to the highway and down through the suburban outskirts. The service was to be held in a glamorous building nestled beside a wide and busy road. Ant parked the car artfully in the empty carpark.

'We're pretty early,' he said.

Inside the building, the ceilings were high and dramatically angled. The perfectly groomed attendants nodded respectfully towards Rattuwat and the younger ones as they entered. A middle-aged woman stepped forward to explain that the body was available for viewing in a small room off the main chapel, and that the family could take as long as they wished to be with the deceased. The children shifted uncomfortably. They did not want to see her. Perhaps they did not know her so well, after all.

'Please, excuse me,' Rattuwat said to the staff, as much as to the children, using the careful English manner he reserved for his clients at the Park Plaza Sukhumvit hotel in Asoke, where he had spent almost ten years as a door attendant.

Rattuwat left the others in the foyer and made his way through a set of heavy, brass-handled doors. In the viewing room, there was a glossy black coffin raised high, centre-front, and before it several empty chairs. He caught sight immediately of the pearl-coloured silk covering the bottom half of his daughter's body. Gradually, he edged forwards until her face came into view.

And there he paused.

Sua had recently celebrated her twenty-seventh birthday; she was practically one-third his age. To Rattuwat, something about her face still held the expression of a child: inquisitive, innocent, accepting. His hands began to shake as he stepped closer to the coffin. He both wanted and did not want to touch his daughter's deathly face. He tried to steel his nerves, but felt his heart beating rapidly against his chest. His whole body seemed to be humming.

The weight of his loneliness was clear to him there in that room as he stood before his daughter's body. A part of him was grateful that the other members of the family were spared this vision of their beloved. As it was, he and Thawin would need to spend another five years paying off the moneylender from Klong Toey who had paid for Rattuwat's single airfare to Perth. But nothing, not even the company of his wife, could have allayed the deep sorrow he felt as he stood before his daughter's open coffin. It was no doubt his own peculiar karmic inheritance to have to bury his firstborn child in this way, but that knowledge did not make it any easier. His gaze was locked on Sua's placid, quiet face and he felt compelled to speak to her, but something held him back. He did not want to call her back, to trap her spirit in the half-world of ghosts. And yet, he longed to hear her voice, and for her to know that he had come. He opened his mouth but no words came out.

It was five years since she had left Bangkok. He stared at the still mask of her face, forced himself to acknowledge it for what it was: a skull encased in decomposing skin, a corpse, no less. This, before him, was his daughter no longer.

He retrieved the photograph he had found yesterday from the inside pocket of his suit, and balanced it carefully against one of the coffin's pewter handles. He turned, then, and sat down in the nearest chair. At home, they would have held the body in their own house, the place would have been noisy with the laughter and feasting of visitors all week long. There would not have been such an empty room, nor this air of quiet sadness and regret.

He sat for a while, eyes closed. Time passed. Then the humming beneath his skin returned. The hairs on the back of his neck began to tingle. Was she aware of him?

'Go,' he whispered. 'You have died, Juum. I am here to see you off. Don't linger now. I give you my permission; I give you my blessing. Go.'

Rattuwat felt in his trouser pocket for the little pieces of paper his wife had pressed into his hand before he left home. On each small square she had carefully written one of four syllables: *ci, ce, ru,* and *ni.* Traditionally, one was to place these inside the mouth of a dying person, to help to focus their mind on the Dharma as the moment of passing grew near. Their own daughter was already dead, but he had promised Thawin he would deliver the little syllables anyway; a belated message from mother to daughter. His palms were sweating as he stood and approached the coffin once more. An unearthly stillness fell in the room. As he bent over the corpse, trembling, the heavy doors to the foyer suddenly burst open and Rattuwat felt a rush of cold air against his skin. The paper syllables scattered on the carpeted floor.

The man from the photograph was standing at the door. His eyes were the same cool blue as the little girl,

Amanda. Rattuwat opened his mouth to speak, but thought better of it. He lowered his eyes, half-nodded at the visitor, and resumed his seat in the nearest row of plushly upholstered chairs, looking at the mess of Thawin's syllables on the floor beneath the coffin.

The Australian took his movement as the signal to move inside and Rattuwat lowered his eyes and listened to the shuffle of the other man's shoes on the soft carpet. He did not want to leave the room, to leave the stranger alone with his daughter's corpse. He kept as still as a mountain, and glimpsed the unwelcome knowledge that he had been trying to deny since he first stepped off the plane: Sua's letters home, so lovingly transcribed, month after month, were a falsehood. She had been telling him and Thawin the things she thought they might like to hear. Further, the children who inhabited her home were not her own.

A new sound entered the room, and it took Rattuwat some time to register that it was the sound of the Australian crying. The old man pressed his lips together in disapproval. He wished the tears to stop. He did not want his daughter called back once more. But he was no more capable of preventing the Australian's grief than he was of bringing his only daughter back to life.

He sat. A few feet in front of him, the Australian wept. The two men remained this way until such time as the heavy foyer doors swung open once more and the boy, Ant, entered.

'Dad,' he said. 'Everyone is waiting.'

It was time to enter the chapel.

There were no monks present at the service.

Rattuwat scanned the faces of the congregation. They were all farang, and many of them poorly groomed. Some had brought their children with them, but there was no Chloe and no Michael. Was one of these families harbouring the real grandchildren? Were they living in someone else's house? Surely the photographs still placed beneath the family shrine at home in Bangkok, surely these were photographs of somebody's flesh-and-blood children. And what, after all, had happened to their father, the man who presented himself to Rattuwat in Bangkok five years ago, to ask for his daughter's hand? His chest ached. It seemed he and Thawin had lost three family members at once.

Rattuwat stood stiffly, militarily, in the front row beside Dave right through the formalities of the service. At the front of the room a man whose accent he had trouble deciphering talked in an abstract manner about celebrating life. Rattuwat drifted in and out of his own thoughts, sometimes giving up on any attempt to translate what the speaker was saying. His chest went on aching. His eyes were dry. But he couldn't help noticing the constant stream of tears coming from the girl in the red dress. She keened and sniffled, wiping mucus all over the back of her hand. Watching her caused Rattuwat physical pain. In some way he had yet to fully understand, that little girl surely belonged to Sua.

CHAPTER FIVE
WHAT KIND OF MOTHER?

The last time Dave saw Amanda's real mother, it was the spring of 2003. He was at a party in Chidlow. He remembered the band, a three-piece, and how it was playing some kind of never-ending improvisation. There was a bloke on bongo drums, a woman on harp, a guitar player on god-only-knows what. It sounded like a mess but occasionally they'd hit a slapdash rhythm that had the fellas tapping their feet, the women swinging their hips. Dave had spent a whole season working with Adie and a few other blokes; they'd been picking mandarins together out at Jude's farm in Gidgegannup. They'd been behaving themselves. And now Adie was throwing a party because they'd all come home again and they had their pockets full of cash and they'd barely touched a drop in five weeks.

Adie's house was an old logger's cottage. The two front rooms were a beautiful coffee-stone job, put together by the local Italian stonemasons before the war. At the back, the place turned into a maze of plasterboard shapes slapped together under a low sloping roof. The night was cool and people had congregated around the fires, two inside and one right down the back, where a pit had been carved into the cold ground and heavily coated figures sat low atop log stools.

Dave had been sitting with the fellas outside, clutching a stainless steel flask of whisky and listening to Pinko as he hammed up a story about the ghost of some logger who'd hung himself from a doorframe, two streets away, in 1933.

The Maggie South who'd sauntered up to him at Adie's place seven years ago was a different Maggie to the one he'd started writing to just recently from prison. The Maggie of seven years ago couldn't even walk straight. She was a small woman, with a mane of beautiful curly hair that fell all the way down her back. But her jaw was locked hard and her face had the yellow pallor of an alcoholic.

The ghost story wasn't yet finished, the speaker just getting to the point where his voice was drawing out the vowels to heighten the suspense, but there was a noise from the direction of the house, some kind of commotion, and a dark figure tumbled out of the back door.

'Ah, fuck off.'

The figure came towards them, half-tripping down the slope of the yard, drunken and swaying.

'Where's the cunt?' Maggie South's voice was loud and shrill and tinged with the sort of emotional despair reserved for those on the very edge of sanity. 'Come here, you cunt!'

'Who's this?' someone replied, and the yarn Pinko was spinning stopped short as people turned to face the new arrival.

'Dave Loos, you arsehole, where are you?'

Dave turned to see a woman swaying in the half-light from the fire, her long grey jacket dragging along the ground and her silhouette misshapen, as if she had a cache of weapons or some kind of contraband hidden beneath her coat. Maggie South stepped towards the orange glow of the pit fire and people moved aside to make way.

'Who wants to know?' said Dave.

'What, you don't want to know me now, eh?'

The group around the fireplace fell silent. Their attention was resting on Dave, who shifted uncomfortably on his stool.

'Easter, last year, Dave. Down at the river, under the fuckin' railway bridge. You remember me now, don't you, you bastard?'

'I don't know what you're talking about.'

'Ha!' Maggie South laughed and there was the sound of some kind of animal coming from beneath her jacket. Dave's stomach was turning and he felt a pang of fear as the form beneath the jacket squirmed and a baby's legs appeared, freed from beneath the woman's coat. With a few swift moves, the woman unbuttoned the front of the long jacket and two wide blue eyes appeared, looking straight at Dave. 'Yeah, take a good look, mate. She's yours. You can fucking have her, too, she's a pain in the arse.' The child's whimper turned into a wail.

'I think you've got the wrong bloke,' said Dave, and people around the fireplace began to murmur.

'Yeah, that'd be right. Too ashamed in front of your mates.'

Adie's wife Susie stood up from her stool and moved towards Maggie South.

'Sweetheart,' she said. 'Why don't you come and sit down. We can talk it out.' She held her hand out for the child.

'Fuck off, you silly bitch. I don't need your fuckin' help.'

Dave looked at the baby's smooth round head, the golden tufts of hair, and then looked away. He remembered a night at the river and a bottle of bourbon and a full moon. But that Maggie South had been different: peaceful, even beautiful, nothing like this.

'How do you know it's mine?' he said and a couple of the fellas beside him laughed.

Maggie fumbled in her pocket and held out something small and shiny. She pushed it under his nose. 'Remember this?'

Dave saw the piece of jewellery and swallowed. He shook his head. She was holding out an eighteen carat gold necklace his mother had given him for his twenty-first birthday. It had a little gold dog tag at the catch with his name and date of birth engraved on it. He hadn't seen it for ages.

'You've got to take her,' said the woman and held the

baby out to him. The child was screaming and smelt of shit. Dave shifted his stool back an inch and kept his hands at his side. 'You've got to take her, man. I'm fucking desperate here.'

He looked away.

People started to murmur again. Nobody knew Maggie South; she wasn't from here. Susie went back to her stool, casting a look at Dave.

'I've never seen you before,' he said and looked into the fire.

Maggie South was close to the edge of something terrible, but she was not a weak woman. She shuffled and turned away. 'There's only two of us here who know the fuckin' truth,' she said. There was a moment of indecision, perhaps. She was heading one way, then another, swaying on her feet. Someone coughed. Someone stoked the fire. Suddenly Maggie swivelled and turned to face him directly.

The baby, Amanda, was barely nine months old, but she was a tiny girl, smaller than she should have been. And her skin was a funny colour. She was sickly.

What Maggie did next was unfathomable. She was a force, all right. Dave watched as Maggie adjusted the weight of the child in her arms, then seized her by the foot and threw her up into the air. What kind of mother would do such a thing to her own child? Dave knew that people in Chidlow would ask this question of each other whenever the girl walked by. They would go on asking it for years. What kind of mother?

It was the sight of the child midair that Dave himself

remembered more than anything: baby Amanda, undersize, underweight, and enclosed in an ill-fitting grow-suit. Her tiny legs were bent as if sitting cross-legged in the dark space of night above the fire pit and she was looking down at him, wide-eyed. I am yours, she said to him, without the need for language, and Dave stood up and caught her while her mother walked away.

Dave took the baby back to the little cottage he'd just started to rent down the road from Adie's in Chidlow. It was just the two of them. He curbed his drinking and went on the single-parent pension. All the time the child raged at him. She screamed at him for forty minutes at a time. She wouldn't sleep at night. She flung her porridge on the floor, chewed on his wallet, pulled at his hair. Dave barely had the stamina for her, couldn't find the patience. He let out a long low sigh every time he had to get up out of bed to go to her. For the first time in his life taking an ordinary job seemed like a good idea; at least it would be a reprieve from what was going on at home. One night after a screaming fit in the bath, he smacked the child's bottom raw with his bare hand, then left the house, left her wailing wet and naked in her cot. She could shit herself in there for all he cared. He sat on an old log at the back of the block and felt his heart racing in his chest. The sun went down. Roos appeared, on track for their dusk drink down at the creek. Gradually, Dave's pulse slowed. When he went back to the girl, she was whimpering. He wrapped her up and put her on his chest in front of the TV until they both slept.

He took to walking the baby in the pram along the quiet, rural roads near home. Sometimes, lacking sleep, he felt like a placid zombie, sailing through the days, weeks. He cooked. Watched a lot of TV. Ant started to come around more often, too, the chaos of his mother's place not so wonderful anymore. Dave didn't mind it. The boy was a good help. He was company, too.

Sometimes Dave looked up John. Sometimes he left the little one with Ant at night, and he and his mate planned a job together, nothing too risky. Over time, they did this less often. The toddler became a preschooler. Dave took up part-time work at Harvey Norman in Midland.

Then Sua arrived.

Those years with her had fallen through his fingers so lightly he had barely noticed them pass. Sometimes he couldn't remember what it felt like to love her. Only that she filled up all his days and nights. Only that she held his children as if they were her own. There were days as simple as he had ever known, wading in the knee-deep water out at Noble Falls with the kids chasing origami boats down the creek and the little dog circling and yapping. There were barbecues at Bill and Pam's place before they moved to Chiang Mai, the two sets of kids lapping the firebreak on the four-wheeler, Sua dropping ice cubes down the back of Dave's shirt while he turned the steaks. And there was fucking her in the big old wrought iron bed before breakfast, or sometimes in the shower after the kids went to bed, once on a blanket in the back of the ute when the moon was full. Seven billion people in the world and these two, born to different languages, different continents, how had it come to be that their lives should align so fully for three whole years?

When he found that reel of blue electrical wire amongst the treasures in her little suitcase last summer it stopped his heart from beating. To have done it was one thing, but to keep the evidence like that. Why? He placed the reel in the glove box of his ute, drove it to work and back with him for a week, took it out and ran it through his fingers more than once. The inscrutability of material things. Eventually he threw it in the skip bin at the back of Harvey Norman.

Steve Manning was a bit player in a minor city. He took advantage of people who were down on their luck, but he was under the radar, as they say. He'd never been to prison.

Only since the funeral had it occurred to Dave that he may have misunderstood the situation. Maybe she was innocent. He wanted to believe that now. He really wanted to. They should have talked about it. But how do you talk about something that sits like a lump in your throat? How do you talk about fear and jealousy and bitterness and shock? How do you talk about trust, so utterly eroded?

For a while Dave had hoped that Bill and Pam might come through for the kids, maybe come back from

Thailand. They still owned the place in Bentley. It was big enough. He had tried to phone them several times, but their number in Chiang Mai was no longer listed. He ended up, inevitably, with some tele-operator whose polite Thai-English stranded him in a meaningless loop. 'One moment, please ... one moment, sir ... one moment.' And then his cash was spent, and the call was disconnected.

The children had told him, back in September, of how they'd been forced to call an ambulance for Sua. The experience frightened them. Apparently she spent three days in intensive care, down in the city, but as soon as they moved her to a standard ward, and the kids went to visit, she demanded to go home. She was so weak Ant had to carry her to the car. Dave phoned home as soon as he heard. The phone rang out, then rang out again. The third time, by some miracle, she answered.

They both listened to the automated announcement that preceded every phone conversation from prison. Then:

'Hi.'

'Dave. It's you.'

A brittle silence, then:

'Why did you call?'

'The kids tell me you're sick.'

'Nothing you can do.'

'You need proper medical care.'

'I don't want it.'

His chest ached. His eyes began to sting. 'Sua, I'm

sorry. I just didn't ... I couldn't ...' She hung up before he could finish, before he could even start.

He phoned back. He phoned back. He phoned back, but there was never any answer.

CHAPTER SIX
ALL ABOUT MRS BROWN

Amanda couldn't understand what had happened between Sua and her dad since he went to jail. Dad never wanted to speak to Sua when he rang up, and she refused to visit him.

When Amanda asked why, Sua said she didn't know why.

'Well, then, why don't you try and be friends again?'

The question went unanswered.

Amanda and Laura had fights sometimes. Usually it was over something stupid. Last time it was because of the door-knocking game. They'd been playing it in some form or another since they first became friends at kindy.

'Knock, knock, knock.'

'Who's there?'

It was the job of the person inside the cubby to open the door a little, peer out, then slam the door on the visitor just as she got close to the threshold.

'No, sorry, we don't want any milk today.'

'Local, organic!'

'No, thank you.'

'Fresh from the cow!'

'No, not today.'

Lately, they'd outgrown the lower school cubby, so they played the door-knocking game whenever they came to see each other at their real houses. Except last time, Amanda was feeling sort of blue. Dad had finally been sentenced. He got heaps longer than they thought he'd get, and Amanda didn't feel like fighting over nothing. She'd mainly come for a piece of Mrs Brown's hummingbird cake. At the Browns' house, tall blue pots lined the entrance, and a perfectly tuned wind chime acted as a doorbell. Ting, tong, ting. Laura said her mother had *an eye for design*. Well, it was true. Things always looked neat at Laura's house.

'Couldn't be too classy,' Amanda's Dad had once said of Mrs Brown, 'after all, she's shacked up in Chidlow.'

Amanda listened to muffled footsteps padding down the hall. When the door opened a fraction, Laura's face peered out. 'No, sorry, we don't want any milk today.'

Amanda was supposed to lean on the door and force her way in, but Laura was bigger than her, big-boned, her mother said, and since it was essentially a game of force, Amanda always ended up squashed.

'No, not today, thank you,' Laura emphasised, with the dismissive lilt of her mother's polite English accent.

Amanda had wedged a foot in the door, but it was a tenuous, half-hearted hold.

Silence descended.

Something about the look in Laura's eye, glimpsed fleetingly through the crack, made Amanda turn away. She moved back along the polished concrete path to the gate. Tears stung. Laura's front door slammed behind her, then reopened, squeaking.

'Amanda? Amanda, where are you going?'

She was not going to answer.

'Amanda! Don't go all sooky. It's only a game.'

'Fuck off,' Amanda yelled over her shoulder. She'd never said that to anyone before.

The girls didn't speak for ages after that.

Amanda didn't know why her father had left them when he did. It was the last week of the summer holidays, and she had only just started to play in a new bush cubby she and Ant had built into the base of a burnt-out jarrah, just north of the house. Dad had joined some slats of wood to work as a floor, and together Amanda and Ant fashioned a makeshift roof out of melaleuca brushes they had collected from the wetlands near the lake. After the others finished helping, Amanda used long sticks to create a lean-to western wall that blocked out the afternoon sun. That alone took a whole afternoon. Satisfied with the structure, she moved in, using carpet scraps for flooring. It was the perfect place to read *Harry Potter*, or to lie on your back and listen to the flit-flit of tiny birds. Little skinks came to visit her there.

From the cubby she could observe occasional activity in the house. A whistling kettle. A vacuum cleaner.

Sometimes a slightly raised voice, her father's stray guffaw. Sua and Dad didn't often fight. But that day was different.

'What the hell?' He came out the laundry door – squeak, slap! – and waved a coil of wire at Sua, who was hanging out the laundry. 'What the *hell* is this?' Sua dropped her peg bag and emerged from behind an upside down singlet. Amanda caught the look that passed between them.

The next minute Dad was revving his ute, spinning the tyres on the driveway, bursting out the front gate.

'What's up his nose?' Amanda asked one of the skinks, though she hardly expected an answer.

Dad didn't come back that night, or the next. Apparently he'd gone to stay at a mate's place. But he stayed there all that week, and then the whole of the next. School went back, and then in February Amanda came home from the Little Athletics State championships with a virus. Laura's mum had taken them down to the brand new stadium at Perry Lakes to watch some of their club members compete. It was exciting and exhausting all at once. They shouted until they were hoarse, and three of their friends won medals, but at home that night Amanda felt sick. Her whole body was hot and every limb ached. She stayed home from school for two days, sat on the couch and watched all the kids' shows on ABC2, along with replays of *WALL-E*, a Disney Pixar DVD she'd seen twelve or thirteen times already.

'Eeevaaa ... Eeevaaa,' she and Laura loved to croon

like parrots at recess. 'Waaallll-EEE!'

It was a kind of bliss, having an excuse to sit on the couch for so long, drinking homemade lemonade, watching DVDs, wiping her nose periodically. The illness was gone by midweek; but then Sua caught it.

A fleeting summer cold, in Sua's case, became what the doctor would come to call a Severe Bacterial Infection. She began coughing as the sun went down, and carried on deep into the night. At first, Amanda slept unaffected in her own room, the rough music of the cough barely fringing her dreams. But the days rolled by and the air in the house grew heavy and Dad still hadn't come home. Amanda took to sitting at the foot of Dad and Sua's bed, sometimes reading from a favourite book, sometimes telling Sua all about her day at school, what Laura said, what the boys were doing at lunchtime, how Mrs Sweeney reacted when John Simons misbehaved after lunch. Her talking calmed them both, and it seemed to hold Sua's coughing at bay. Later Amanda would wake in a little ball, like a kitten, at the far corner of the big queen bed, a light blanket thrown over her, and she would wonder again about what had gone wrong with Sua and her dad.

Ant was good for a while. He started being home more. Sua gave them her ATM card and the PIN number – 0731 – and they took Dad's unregistered car to Coles in Mundaring and bought the groceries. They filled their trolley with baked beans and spaghetti in cans, pork sausages, lots of apples and bananas, two-minute noodles and frozen peas and corn, sometimes a family-sized block of chocolate.

The nights got cooler, the days shorter, and then they heard that Dad was going to appear in court for something. Sua didn't want the kids to go to the hearing. She took the train into the city by herself.

Nobody wanted to mention the diarrhoea, at first. Amanda figured it would be gone in a few days. But it was not. Sua had always been small and thin, but after ten days of runny poo she reminded Amanda of the frail little finch they had tried unsuccessfully to save the previous spring. There was something about Sua's skin, too: it was changing colour.

'Is your tummy ever going to get better?' Amanda asked one Saturday morning, when Sua rose late and Amanda was already eating toast and honey in front of the television.

'I don't know,' Sua said, and Amanda thought she saw tears forming at the corner of her eyes. She was holding her hand at her stomach, as if to fix something in place.

Sua hardly got out of bed at all, after that.

One school day afternoon during term two, Amanda and Sua took the bus into Midland to see the Indian doctor at the Super Clinic. Sua was leaning heavily on Amanda's arm all the way up from the bus stop and needed to stop every few minutes to rest. Ant had been supposed to drive them but hadn't shown up in time. When Amanda sent him a text, he replied: SRRY FORGOT. CN SHE CHANGE IT 2 2MRW? But Sua said they couldn't change it.

It was windy and wet walking along the highway. And all the people who were driving past were staring at them.

'Fuck-knuckles,' Amanda said, under her breath.

The doctor's waiting room was full. People sniffled and sneezed with early-season infections. Amanda was worried that Sua would catch something from them. She sat staring at the puzzles page in a long out-of-date copy of *TV Week*. Connecting the dots on a picture of an Easter bunny reminded her of an afternoon spent with Ant and Dumpy on the Western Power trail near their house, ages ago, when Dumpy had stunned a rabbit with his slingshot. He'd used a blunt knife from his trouser pocket in an amateur attempt to skin it. It was gross. Eventually the innards came out all white and grey and the boys threw them in a pile in the bush. Then Ant came running at her with his bloody hands. She was running from him screaming, when something wet hit the ground near her ankle. Splat. She looked back to see the rabbit's heart, still thumping. She was stunned. It was a trick she longed to understand. How was it that a heart could go on beating, outside of a body, even after an animal was dead?

Sua always wanted her to come into the doctor's consultation room with her; she didn't like to be alone with a strange man. But this time, when they got there, the doctor asked whether it would not be better to ask the child to leave the room.

'The girl is okay. She knows already,' Sua said, her grip tight on Amanda's wrist.

Amanda smiled apologetically at the doctor, her face burning with embarrassment. 'Don't worry,' she said, 'I won't listen.' The doctor stared blankly back at her for a moment, then directed the rest of the discussion towards Sua.

'Very well. I must tell you,' he said, 'the blood results are not good. This is why I wanted you to come in person. I would like to arrange for you to go into hospital immediately. We need to do an up-to-date CD4 count, calculate your viral load, test for opportunal infections. There are drugs we can put you on to significantly inhibit the progress of the disease. You need to begin with these straight away. To be honest with you, Mrs Brown, I don't know how it is that you have been able to cope at home. You are very ill.'

Amanda swallowed and looked up at Sua, whose face was flat, her gaze steadfastly in her own lap. Why was he calling her Mrs Brown?

That night, Sua feigned wellness. She ate at the table, and sat up for a while afterwards, coaching Amanda on how to carve a carnation out of a radish. They cut it into two pieces. At the slender end, they carved grooves along the length, then a series of thin, full petals. Sua shaped each petal with one swift movement, a simple flick.

'You make it look so easy,' Amanda complained. Hers didn't look right.

'I learned a long time ago.'

'I can't do it.'

'You must practise.'

Sua corrected the petals on one of Amanda's abandoned pieces.

'What made you come to Australia?' Amanda asked.

'A man said he loved me. I thought I loved him too.'

'You don't mean Dad?'

'No. Before I met your dad.'

'What happened?'

Sua's finished carvings were milky and delicate, the radishes utterly transformed. She placed them on a plate in the middle of the table and sat back in her chair.

'Men can be cruel,' she said.

'How do you mean?'

'I believed he loved me. He said we would get married.'

Sua's voice changed. Amanda tried to meet her eyes again, but Sua was looking away.

'He had a hard heart,' she said. 'We lived together, he had a house in Stirling. But he always watched me. He didn't let me leave the house without him.'

'What did he think you were going to do?'

'I don't know. Actually, he started to lock me in there when he went to work.'

'Lock you where?'

'In the house.'

'What did you do?'

'I watched TV. Got better at English that way. Watched all day and night.'

A ghostly, half-imagined shape loomed at the edges of Amanda's vision. Was there something there? She shivered.

'No, I mean, how did you get away from him?'

'By accident,' Sua laughed. 'He had an accident.'

After dinner they sat in Sua and Dad's bed together, and got out the colouring books.

Then Sua told her one of the old Thai stories her mother used to tell her as a girl. It was a story about men and women and love, and Sua told it with her eyes shut, like she knew it inside out. The tale began with a wealthy man and his concubine in the times of kings and queens. One day, a handsome robber came along. The robber had developed a reputation for stealing from the rich and sharing some of his takings with the poor. He was very good at it, too. He was notorious. The king of the land ordered his soldiers to track down the robber and bring him before him. There was a great public campaign, with huge rewards offered. Shortly afterwards the robber was captured and paraded through the streets. He was to be killed at a public event the next day. But when the robber was paraded past the concubine, who watched from a high balcony, something extraordinary happened. She fell in love with him. It was love at first sight. She knew already what was destined for him and she couldn't bear it. So she connived with her patron to have the robber rescued from the prison overnight, and for someone else to die in his place.

This was what happened, but not quite in the way the wealthy man had planned. The next day the concubine fled with her new lover, the robber, to a little-known house in the country. And the wealthy man who had loved her for many years, and kept her in such a fine clothes, was the one put to death in his place. The concubine had tricked him. She and the robber lived happily together for several years, Sua said, until one day he discovered the truth about what had happened to the other man. Then, he couldn't stand to be with his lover anymore. He began to fear her. What of her next whim? If someone else were to catch her attention in the way he had, it would be his turn to walk into one of her traps. She was treacherous. But he loved her. What could he do? He decided to leave her. And she was heartbroken for the rest of her days.

Amanda shaded carefully between the lines of a mandala with Imperial Purple. The story was cruel. All the characters were cruel. Even the wealthy man, who died. He shouldn't have kept the woman like a slave.

The days passed. Sua's health weakened further. Amanda went to school less often.

'Could be worse,' Amanda heard Sua telling her friend Pam on the phone to Thailand one morning. 'I do not live on the street.'

As Amanda sat scraping the dirt from beneath her fingernails, a thought fell into place. All those visits to the doctor as Mrs Brown. Sua had stolen Laura's mother's name.

CHAPTER SEVEN
HE LOST HER TWICE

That little baby girl of his – the one who was dead now – he still remembered precisely how small she was when she was born, the length of her no greater than his own forearm. She came nearly two weeks later than predicted, and she did so back-to-front, causing her mother a long and painful labour. When Rattuwat held his daughter for the first time he pulled aside the soft white muslin wrap and retrieved her hand. She wrapped her fingers around one of his as he looked closely into her red and angry face. Rattuwat had come to parenting at a mature age, already into his fifties, but when he looked at that baby's face he felt a sense of awe that he had never felt before. It seemed the girl knew already something of what life was about. And while she had put up what resistance she could during the labour, it was the only tantrum she ever had. Rattuwat gave her the nickname Juum, meaning splash, because she had arrived so dramatically, but thereafter settled quickly into peacefulness. Within weeks she was sleeping and feeding in a predictable pattern that came to foreshadow her placid and good-natured approach to everyday life. She rarely cried.

Their neighbourhood in Ubon Ratchathani marvelled for years about the time when Sua was three years old, and she was trampled by an angry buffalo, leaving her with fierce bruising and a broken wrist. Afterwards, she simply picked herself up from the ground and wiped the dirt from her hands. '*Pôr*,' she said, looking up at her father, 'I hurt me.' There were no tears.

Rattuwat and Thawin had kept every letter, every postcard their adult daughter had sent to them from Australia. The collection was piled into a small cardboard box in their single room in the modern-style multistorey building they had moved into after the children had left. And though he was now struggling to find any truth at all to the quaint domestic narrative his daughter had wanted him and her mother to believe, he still felt nervous to think of that little bundle of papers, so far away. He was itching to read them all over again, to look for clues between the lines. His daughter's handwriting was neat and careful, the paper lightweight and pale blue, the kind reserved for airmail. It was all they had left of her now.

Perhaps, for all his doting, he had not been the most careful of fathers.

In 1997, they were still living above the family whitegoods business in Ubon Ratchathani. If not for the financial crisis of the late nineties, they might still be there now, his brother, their two wives, the children and grandchildren. It was a dream Rattuwat indulged in occasionally. In fact, he knew that if had he not left the bulk of the financial decisions to his brother in the first place, they might have got through even that period. Proi was a risk-taker. That was always clear. But the scale of his risk-taking went unnoticed for too many years. When the stock market floundered in the capital, Rattuwat made the trip to Bangkok to try to ensure supply of their stock from a trader whose father had once been a close friend of their own. When he got there, he discovered the truth: the entire value of the business had been fully mortgaged for some years, and the stocks Proi had gambled on were worthless. Their company was 1.3 million baht in debt. But that was not the worst of it. Within days of Rattuwat's discovery, Proi was dead.

When Rattuwat got home to Ubon, already burdened with the news of his brother's suicide, he witnessed a more confounding sense of loss on the face of his own wife.

'Juum has disappeared,' she told him.

'What do you mean? How could she have disappeared?'

'Two days ago. She helped me prepare the first meal, she never came to the second.'

'How could she disappear between the house and the school? There is only a few blocks to walk. Everybody knows her there. Where did you look?'

'I have looked. Everybody has looked. She is nowhere.'

For Rattuwat and his wife, those three years between 1997 and 2000 were the longest years of their married life. Bankrupt and heartbroken, they moved back to Warin Chamrap, the village in which Rattuwat's parents were born, and lived with his peasant cousins, fourteen family members in a one-room house. Daily life was reduced to a dull and exhausting pattern of physical labour in the fields. Rattuwat and Thawin withdrew from each other and from their sons, Arthit and Lek, each carrying out their daily work with a solemnity that was new to their once lighthearted family. Juum's name was barely spoken between them: they struggled just to carry on, to save face. Rattuwat went more regularly to the nearby forest monastery to speak to the head monk, who gave him the same simple advice about the eight winds, the eight conditions and the value of non-attachment he had been giving him all his life. In the third year, at the Bun Bang Fai festival, Rattuwat and Thawin got drunk together and broke their silence about their daughter. They talked for a long time about everything that had happened, and they decided to release a bird for Juum; it was a traditional gesture, aimed at setting her spirit free. Even if it would not bring Sua back, perhaps it would help to cure their unhappiness, or to lighten the impact of their poverty. They arranged it with the bird handler, and Rattuwat felt a weight shift from his shoulders as soon as the white bird fled its cage. A glance across at Thawin and he knew that she felt the same.

The following afternoon, a teenager in blue jeans, carrying a small handbag, stepped off the *songthaew* from Ubon. It was Sua.

The girl who stepped back into Rattuwat's family that May was different to the one they'd known three years earlier. Her body had become the body of a young woman, and she was beautiful, despite the awful Western-style clothes. But it was her face that struck them as so different. Her expression revealed immediately to Rattuwat that she had seen too much. She held her head up high all the way along the dirt lane to her paternal grandmother's house, but when she knelt in front of her parents on the old grass mat upstairs, she burst into tears.

It took years to find out the truth about what had happened. If Rattuwat had been given access to the facts in 1997 he could probably have saved Sua from those years. He could have tracked her down, somehow, bargained her back. But the cruelty was this: of all the rumours that reached his family's ears during that time in the old village, none of them steered anywhere near the truth. The day before he died, Rattuwat's brother had traded his niece to people traffickers to settle a personal debt. As it turned out, everybody in their old district knew, but nobody had the courage to mention it directly to Rattuwat and his wife.

They lost her again in 2005, not long after Rattuwat found himself sitting across from the big Australian man – Steve – at the makeshift tables beside their local noodle seller in Bangkok. Steve was not well dressed. His singlet, with great armholes, showed half his torso, and his baggy shorts, a faded khaki green, had a large ink stain on the left pocket. He wore flip-flops. Was this any way to dress to meet your potential father-in-law?

'She is a good daughter,' he said to the Australian. '*Lôok săao dee.*'

'Don't worry, mate,' said Steve. 'I look after girl.' He grinned broadly and nodded, pointing to himself and then at Sua. 'I look after girl.'

Rattuwat looked away, embarrassed.

This was not what he and Thawin had in mind for their only daughter. The family had been living in Bangkok almost a full year, and Sua had a good job at the cosmetics counter at the big retailer MBK. She was happy there. Nobody here knew anything about the stolen years. The twins, too, were happy in their new roles with the local *motorcy* gang, ferrying the local commuters up and down the *soi*, every day a game of strategy and chance, a kind of sport. But now, here was the Australian man, eager to split the five of them up.

Rattuwat watched sweat forming on Steve Manning's brow and thought it unlikely that any good would come of the marriage. Most of the men in their neighbourhood would consider it a blessing to have a daughter good-looking enough to draw the attentions of a rich farang, to have one of the family put down roots in a Western country like Australia, but Rattuwat watched the Australian carefully across the table and could see no reason to rejoice.

And yet it was what she wanted, the girl. It was all she talked about. Rattuwat could not bring himself to disappoint her.

When the day came to leave for the airport, Thawin could not bear to go to wave them off. She did not even want to witness Sua packing her clothes into the small black suitcase-on-wheels which the Australian had given her. She sat on their shared bed watching the television.

Rattuwat and the boys rode with Sua and the Australian to Don Muang Airport in the metered taxi. While they waited in the traffic on the Vibhavadi Road, Rattuwat took off one of several amulets that hung around his neck and held it forth in both hands, nodding at his daughter.

'This was my grandmother's,' he said.

Sua took the amulet in both hands while her brothers looked on. It was a tiny buddha carved in tiger tooth, mounted inside a small silver and glass case. It was the most valuable thing their family now owned.

'For protection.'

'*Pôr*, this is yours,' she said, 'you need it for yourself.'

'Take it. You don't know what can happen in a foreign country. You are still young, Juum. You need plenty of luck.'

Rattuwat looked his daughter in the eye. He found himself unable to interpret her expression. Was she sad or happy? Was she sure about what she was doing? This was to be the last time he would ever see her alive, and a part of him sensed it, even then.

'You are a good daughter,' he said to her. 'A good daughter.'

After Sua left, Rattuwat sometimes allowed himself to imagine that her marriage to the farang would mean a move to Australia for himself and Thawin; that they might live out their old age in their son-in-law's first-world house, Sua tending to them in their frailty, they, in turn, lending their wisdom to the grandchildren. His Isaan friends, living in Bangkok, encouraged this fantasy, indeed they believed it the chief reason for seeking out such a marriage for any eligible daughter. It was perhaps this foolish but persistent daydream that had allowed him and his wife to loosen up on the supervision of their sons, to fail to pay the right sort of attention when the boys became distant and moody. Rattuwat could not put his finger on the precise day or week or month he lost his boys to the slum gang. If he had been aware of it, he might have moved more swiftly to prevent the situation. If he had been aware of it, he would never have let them go.

'The door to my house is always open to you,' he had often promised his children. And it was true: the door was open. But the children chose to walk through it less and less.

When he took the urgent phonecall from the Australian – the second Australian, Dave – and registered the news of his daughter's death, Rattuwat walked away from his post at Park Plaza Sukhumvit and went immediately in search of the twins at the headquarters of the outlaw *motorcy* gang buried deep in the slums of Kloeng Toey. It was a risk even to walk those narrow dirt streets in that neighbourhood, and he was threatened by several gatekeepers, and by a volley of dogs, but he needed the boys to know, and further, for them to be with him when he broke the news to their mother. When Arthit and Lek finally appeared in the doorway of a makeshift hovel, Rattuwat could see from the look in their eyes that they were no longer completely human. The boys were twin ghosts. There was barely the slightest recognition at the name of their sister; the word death meant even less to them. They refused to come home.

From his position beneath the ancient Australian tree, surveying the dry, salt-pocked farming land, Rattuwat tasted only regret. He should have done more to fight for his children, all of them. He supposed he had trusted them to find their own way, make their own mistakes. He had never sought to control them in the manner of his own father. Now he wondered whether that approach was a poor excuse for laziness. In his mind, he heard again the distant voice of Vithi, son of the politician for whom Rattuwat had worked as a driver in Bangkok during his youth.

'You people from Isaan, you are put to work like dogs,' Vithi said to Rattuwat once, catching his eye in the rear-view mirror as he sat on the softly upholstered leather seat of his father's luxury car. 'Listen comrade, you see the slums here in Bangkok, they are full of farming people. Our people, Thai people, are starving right here in the capital, while the ruling class get fat on English teacake, looking ridiculous in those cheap Western suits.'

Rattuwat didn't always know how to respond to Vithi. He did not want to cause any trouble. Most of the time he said nothing.

'You see? You see how you are?' the university student would chide him. 'How can you improve your people's lot when you are so passive? This is the problem with our country. Somebody shits in our cooking pot, right in the middle of our house, and all we can do is kneel down and *wai* to them in gratitude.'

Once, Rattuwat quoted the Buddha to him: 'Holding on to anger is like grasping a hot coal.'

Vithi scoffed. 'It is so convenient isn't it? Have you ever thought about that? The Dharma tells us not to get angry, no matter what the ruling dictators choose to do to us. In this fashion, we are docile. We are too easy to manipulate. No, we are fools.'

Remembering this now, Rattuwat shook his head. Poor Vithi. He was the first real communist Rattuwat had ever met. And he was long dead now: shot dead by Field Marshal Sarit's men in 1963. Four decades had passed and the young man's voice still followed his one-time chauffeur around.

Actually, right now, Rattuwat was almost as destitute as he had been in the fifties, in the days before he took the job driving for Vithi's father. Two days ago, he had changed his last two thousand baht at the airport in Bangkok. It amounted to fifty Australian dollars. Half of this he had spent yesterday at the little supermarket near his son-in-law's house. He had bought flowers for the makeshift altar to his daughter that he had set up in the main room of the cottage, and then he had bought food for himself and the little girl. Now, he had a little less than twenty Australian dollars in his pocket. If he could not find his way back to the car, to the girl, to the little house in the paddock in which his daughter had spent her last years, he might even die here himself.

For the first time since the dim days of the nineteen seventies – six years he spent in a prison camp by the Mekong River – Rattuwat felt almost completely bereft of hope. He longed for the company of his wife, the touch of her nose against his. He looked up at the sun and envied its relentless strength. I have failed each and every one of my children, he thought. And then he gazed across the dry paddock and noticed a farm tractor, edging the perimeter. So, there was life here, after all. He stood, as carefully as he could, and waved his arms in the direction of the farmer.

'Hello?' he called. 'Hello!'

But he might as well have been made from glass. The tractor turned the corner of the paddock and receded into the distance.

CHAPTER EIGHT
WHAT ABOUT THE GIRL?

It was almost one o'clock. For the second time that day, Dave sat on the long bench in the crowded holding bay outside the visitors centre, waiting for his name to come up. He didn't feel up to making eye contact with the other cons; to them it was any other Sunday afternoon and they seemed to him to be unnecessarily jovial. He concentrated on bouncing his heel and watching his knee jitter, until the screw with the hook nose shouted his surname, running it together with 'Table 31'. And then Dave was let loose into the cavernous hall, empty of furnishings but for several neat rows of MDF tables and chairs bolted to the floor, a few stray snack machines.

Table 31 was right up the far end, near the Coke machine. A few of the other prisoners had overtaken him from behind, eager to see family members or lovers, and Dave observed a couple kissing, a baby being passed to his father. His own steps towards the designated table were more cautious.

When he gained the confidence to look straight at the woman seated there, he recognised Amanda's mother immediately. She looked okay, and he was kind of surprised to acknowledge it. She looked better than he had thought she would, in a long Indian skirt and a close-fitting blue singlet top. No jewellery; they take that off at reception. Her hair was still long, and its natural colour, a dusty blonde. She looked well. And then he wondered what he must look like from her point of view. She was still gazing in the direction of the prisoners' entrance. Clearly, she hadn't recognised him yet. What part of the old Dave was missing, he wondered, what telltale sign?

As he got closer it became clear that he had her table in mind to sit at and so she was forced to look directly at him, to assess him. She stood. If she was happy or unhappy to see him, it didn't show.

'Hi,' she said, and leaned across the table to kiss him, awkwardly, on the cheek.

'This is embarrassing,' he said, blushing.

Dave's knee was still bouncing up and down beneath the table as they started to talk. Theirs was an awkward to and fro, punctuated with pauses and stutters and efforts to be polite which, under the circumstances, seemed a waste of time. The fact was that he and Maggie South barely knew each other. He'd run into a bloke in J Unit three months ago who turned out to be Maggie's brother. Dave told him the story, discovered Maggie was on the wagon, asked for her address. Then he wrote to her. Twice.

Now he sat across from her and found himself talking about Sua, and he knew he probably shouldn't, but he hadn't talked about Sua to anyone, really, since the funeral, and he needed to. He needed to. Everything he thought Sua's father should know, he told it to Maggie.

'I can't explain it,' he said. 'I just ... something snapped inside me, you know. I couldn't be with her after that. I just thought, Jesus, you know. It could have been me.'

Maggie caught his eye, then looked away. She changed the subject. Asked him about life in prison.

He told her their shared cell was so small that it was possible to stand in the shower and piss into the toilet bowl at the same time. She laughed at this and it softened her face. He found himself smiling back. Then he filled her in on Lofty, in for armed robbery, same as him. 'Hey,' he said, 'at least we've got one thing in common.'

He told her about the kind of work that was available inside: there was a toy workshop, a metal workshop, a carpentry workshop, a laundry. He had an afternoon job in the kitchen, he told her. It passed the time.

'Bet you know plenty of people in here from the old days, hey?' she said.

'No, actually,' he said.

She seemed unconvinced.

'I keep to myself. Most days, I spend an hour or two in the gym of a morning, come back to the cell for a bit, watch a movie, then start my shift in the kitchen. I buy the paper once a week. Read a bit. Right now, I'm reading this sci-fi thing, it's a graphic novel.'

'A comic book?' she laughed.

'Nah, piss off.'

'We get three movie channels here. I saw *Gone With the Wind* one night.'

Maggie had once declared it her all-time favourite film. Actually, Dave thought it was shit, and he told her as much, but the fact that he'd raised the topic at all was an admission, of sorts. It was his way of acknowledging a conversation they shared, beneath a railway bridge, almost nine years ago.

They smiled at each other and it seemed to him that they were getting along okay.

But after that, no matter where Maggie tried to steer the conversation, Dave kept on coming back to Sua and he knew he shouldn't have and he struggled not to, but his head was so full of her these last days.

'I swear to God, if I'd just known she was going to get so sick, I never would have walked away.'

Maggie asked about his son.

'Nearly eighteen. Keeping his nose out of trouble, as far as I know. Not that you can know, especially from here. I just wish he was eighteen already. If he was, I wouldn't have to go through all this bullshit over the custody of the little one.'

Maggie didn't so much as flinch at the reference to Amanda. It was like it hadn't even registered. This bothered him.

'You ever dream about getting out?' she asked him.

He sighed. 'Hell, yeah. I sit here in my cell, sometimes, like any con, I guess, and dream up grand escape plans.'

'Such as?'

'You think I'd tell you if I had one?' He grinned at her. 'Anyway, it's a pipedream. Nobody has ever escaped from here. The place is brand new, and it's as high-tech as they get. Built for high security, even though it's only classified as medium.'

He showed Maggie his dog tag, a thin piece of plastic with a chip in it; something that told the screws exactly which area a convict was in at any given moment of the day or night. He told her how they used eye-scans to divvy out medications. 'So they can tell exactly who you are,' he said, 'before they give it to you. If somebody is missing, they issue a Code Red and they lock us all down and go over the place with a fine toothcomb until they find him. The only way to get out of here would be with something like a chopper. Fly in, fly out, like that bloke in Sydney did. Land it on the oval. You could probably get a desperate farmer to do it, you know those blokes on the big stations up north that use helicopters to round up their cattle?'

You heard stories all the time. Apparently a guy tried to scale the perimeter fence at Canning Vale once. 'They shot him. His body got so tangled up in the wires it took them three days to get him down. The crows got stuck into him.'

'What about if you knew someone,' she suggested, 'one of the screws. What about bribes?'

'Most popular method is the old garbage truck trick,' Dave cut across her. It was a good and familiar game.

'That's a bit obvious, isn't it? They'd see you a mile away.'

'Just a few weeks ago, a fella climbed into the driver's seat of a garbo truck over at Wooroloo and drove it clear through the perimeter fence. Still ain't found 'im.'

They were interrupted by the public address system and an announcement signalling the end of the first half of the session. People could leave now, if they wanted. A few of the other visitors were already standing up to go. Their shoes squeaked on the shiny gymnasium floor. Dave glanced nervously around the room as Maggie, too, stood up.

'You don't have to go yet,' he said. She didn't understand. They could have an extra thirty minutes if they wanted.

'Dave, I'm sorry,' she said, placing a shaky hand on his arm, 'this place is making me nervous.'

He stood up to plead with her. She pecked him on the cheek again.

'We haven't even talked about the girl,' he said, trying not to raise his voice. He couldn't believe it. She was actually leaving early. It wasn't meant to be like this. They needed to make a decision. Besides, he'd already set Amanda up to expect something. But the silly bitch was running scared already.

'Maybe you could come back next week?' he asked her.

'You want me to come back?' she said.

'Of course I bloody do.'

'I'll see.'

What had he said? She was backing off.

'What about Amanda?' he asked again, conscious of the anxious tone that had crept into his voice.

'I don't know. I've only just come good myself, Dave.'

She was leaving. He couldn't help it that his voice was getting louder.

'Just wait.'

Now the hook-nosed screw was on his way over. People at the nearby tables were staring.

'Haven't you got anybody else to ask?' she said.

He looked Maggie South in the eye, squinting at her, and anger coursed through him. 'No!' he said. 'I don't! *We don't.* That's the whole fucking point!'

Dave had to wait back in the holding pen for the rest of the cons to finish before he could go back to his unit. He sat rigid and when the others finally came along and the bunch of them was shifted back through Movement Control, he stopped short of making eye contact with anyone. His fingers were itching to roll himself a smoke, but he had no tobacco left and he wasn't in the mood for cadging one.

'Haven't you got anybody else to ask?' the bitch had said, as if this were another unbelievable failing on his part, as if she had nothing to do with any of it.

It was true that he and Sua had withdrawn from people a little these past few years. They wanted a normal life, well, to the extent that you could have a normal life, as an ex-con and a non-citizen. But it worked for them, it just did. Dave took on some extra hours down at Harvey Norman. Sua cooked and cleaned and drove the kids to and from school. He bought that dog-wash van for her, a good little cash business. She was going to do it on weekends. They were settled, each of them, for the first time in their adult lives. There was a joy to that, fragile, but almost tangible. Then he found the blue electrical wire.

Anger flared in him.

When Dave laid himself down on the mattress in his cell his head was suddenly full of Amanda, her childish high-pitched laugh, the excited glint in her eye. He wanted to stay with the memory of her, but her presence was laced with something darker. She was his baby one: eight years old and, thanks to him, now at the mercy of the welfare system. He started to cough and his eyes filled with tears. It was rotten that he'd just spent nearly half an hour with the child's natural mother and neither of them was brave enough to face the issue of their daughter's future head-on.

Dave closed his eyes, imagining Maggie South only half an hour before, walking back to her car, climbing into the driver's seat, turning the key in the ignition. What kind of car, he wondered, and he conjured up a beaten old Holden, stripped bare along one side where somebody had never quite finished the panel-beating job. And she would have a good luck charm, he figured, dangling from her key ring, some kind of American

Indian feather or some shit like that. He swallowed hard and saw the woman's heart-shaped face again. It was the same shape as his daughter's.

The shame he had felt when Maggie first looked across the table at him was billowing like a storm cloud inside his head. 'How do you know it's mine?' he'd jeered at her, all those years ago, sitting around the fire at Adie's place. He wanted to die. The fact was he was a shit father, a low-life piece of scum, and the only woman he'd ever loved was dead. Even Maggie fucking South, the mad bitch, even she looked good, compared to him. At least she'd kept herself out of jail. It was Dave who was the dickhead. He'd let the children down. They needed him and he wasn't there for them and he felt ashamed. It didn't seem possible to face another day, another hour, another breath in this fucked-up cage of steel and concrete they dared to call a Correctional Centre.

He ached for a cigarette. Where the hell was Sua's old man? Where the hell was Amanda? What the fuck were they doing to him?

CHAPTER NINE
SOMETHING MIGHT HAPPEN

Somewhere towards the bottom of the gully a movement caught Amanda's eye. It was a farm tractor, far enough away to resemble a matchbox toy. She watched as a tiny figure stepped down from the cabin to open a gate. If she'd had to colour the scene, she'd have chosen Burnt Yellow Ochre for the base of the gully and Crimson Lake for the tractor.

Only a month ago, Sua had told her that she had to be brave; that she was going to have to witness something girls her age should never have to see; that she was doing a good job. By that stage, Sua was completely refusing to leave the house, even for the doctor. 'What if something happen?' she'd say whenever Amanda suggested it. The girl thought this was a pretty weird thing to say. Something was always happening, even if it was something boring, it was still something.

When Ant went off with his mates and they needed stuff at the shops, Amanda rode her bike into Chidlow and bought frozen dinners or cooked chooks at the local store. She rode a wide berth around the mobile dogwash van that Dad had bought Sua two summers ago. It sat forlorn at the top of the driveway. Weeds were shooting up around the edges of its wheels and cobwebs had taken the reflective sheen off of the rear-view mirrors. Amanda spotted the Nokia that carried the SIM card for the business, abandoned on the front seat, its shape half-melted by the sun.

It was boring being at home all the time.

When she asked Sua if they couldn't just go for a drive, Ant could take them, they wouldn't even need to get out of the car, the answer was still no. 'What about cop on road?' They both knew what could happen. Sua had explained often enough. The immigration cops could catch her anywhere, anytime, she said. But Amanda wondered why it seemed more likely now than it had a few months ago, a year ago, or before Dad went to jail.

In the middle of the facing paddock, a few massive jarrah trees stood gnarled and tall, even though long dead. Their branches were ghostly, useless claws, like the chicken feet Amanda had seen hanging in the window of the Asian grocer in Midland. While she watched, a flurry of cockatoos fled their branches. She moved her gaze along the firebreak and witnessed the rusty crimson tractor drawing closer.

When it arrived, its engine gave a deafening rumble and patter that filled her stomach with dread. While the vehicle idled in a jerky manner, the farmer climbed down from the cab. His bare legs were a wiry plait of muscle. His shirt was stained with sweat.

'You all right?' he said.

He wore those short khaki shorts some of her dad's mates liked to wear. Stubbies, they were called. Amanda sensed he was slightly annoyed by her presence, as if she was costing him time he didn't care to waste.

'Take you up to the house,' he said, as he climbed back into the cab. 'The Missus'll look after you.'

The cab was not really big enough for two and she found it hard to avoid brushing against his bare legs as she stood, one hand on the roll bar, one foot on the uppermost step.

Something might happen, she thought. In the middle distance she could see the bushland she had walked through less than an hour before. Dogs were barking somewhere, a tuneless, repetitive racket.

Beneath the tall trees that surrounded the farmer's house, she made out a small family of kangaroos resting in the shade. One lifted its head, sniffed the air, and took in the sight of the tractor, the man, the child. Suddenly the farmer pressed down on the tractor's horn and a low dull tone broke the peace. Amanda jumped.

'Bloody nuisance animals.'

The Missus tended to Amanda with the calm authority of a woman used to unannounced visitors, as if the traffic of strangers and waifs through her farmhouse kitchen had been a regular theme.

'Come in, love, you can use the phone and let your

mum know where you are,' she'd said. 'I bet she's worried sick.'

When Amanda phoned the number at home, it rang out unanswered. She willed Ant to be there, to pick up the phone, but at the same time she knew that her ability to summon her brother had weakened of late, if indeed she had ever been able to do it. Telepathy was a stupid thing to believe in, anyway, a childish thing. She would give up on trying.

There was no point in phoning the prison. Dad could ring out sometimes, but you couldn't ring in and ask for him. Besides, the visit would have been cancelled hours ago. Dad would be cross.

The farmer's wife placed a plate of scrambled eggs on toast and a big glass of orange juice on the old wooden table. She pulled out a chair.

'Get some food into your tummy, love,' she said. 'You can try the phone again later.'

Amanda ate while the woman fussed about in the big kitchen. She was preparing the Sunday lunch, lamb and potatoes and green beans. They used to have that kind of Sunday roast at Uncle Adie's house when Amanda was little, so different from the sort of cooking Sua had taught her since. Amanda thought, again, of old Rattuwat, sitting in the shade of the firebreak where she'd left him, hours before. She knew the right thing to do was to mention him to The Missus, to have the farmer go and look for him, pick him up. She cleared her throat but then, as the woman glanced at her, she faltered, swallowing a dry corner of toast.

'I could try my brother's mobile,' she said hopefully.

'Yes, you do that, dear,' the woman said.

Amanda was grateful for the woman's matter-of-factness. There had been no interrogation, so far, but the girl knew that it was unlikely to last, especially if she couldn't get through to anyone. She knew Ant's latest mobile number by heart and a spark of optimism flowed through her as she dialled. She could feel her heart beating in her chest. Ant would come and get her in one of Dumpy's cars. They would find the old man together. But before she could speak to her brother the ringtone was cut short by a familiar announcement: *The mobile you are dialling is switched off or out of range. A text message containing the number you are calling from will be sent if you hang up now.* She watched the farmer's wife turning over large pieces of potato on an oven tray and for a moment she considered pretending to speak to Ant. She could invent some fake meeting place for the benefit of the farmer's wife and disappear into the afternoon heat. But just at that moment the woman glanced up at her and smiled and something about her straightforward generosity prevented Amanda from carrying through on her plan. She hung up the phone, her skin prickling with heat. She was blushing.

'I'm sure they're all out looking for you, sweetheart,' said the woman.

Returning the clunky old handset back in its cradle on the kitchen wall, Amanda watched the steam rising from the half-finished plate of eggs.

'Is there something you need to tell me, pet?'

The farmer's wife had pale skin, lightly freckled, and her upper arms were flabby beneath her short-sleeved dress. Amanda could easily imagine those arms wrapped around the several children The Missus must have once had in her care. She wanted for a moment to be comforted in that way, too, but knew already the danger of such women, how they could hold you in a way that made your tears flow strong, and then before you knew it you were telling them more than they needed to know and they, in turn, would have to tell the Appropriate People, as Mrs Brown once put it. Somebody else might come for her then. A tear fell, but Amanda steadied herself and went back to the table and sat down in front of the plate of eggs.

'I'm just a bit tired,' she said.

'Yes, of course you are.'

'I'll try again later.'

'Yes, dear.'

The spare room at the farmer's house held an old-fashioned single bed made out of wrought iron. The bedhead featured a quaint spiral pattern, like something out of a children's book. On the wall there was a framed picture of a farm scene, a wheat harvest baled and turning pink in the sunset. The place smelt faintly of mothballs.

Amanda felt babyish having a lie down during the daytime, but at the same time she was exhausted. Her skin was dry and hot with sunburn and her legs ached. The plan was not to fall asleep, but just to lie quietly for a while, as the farmer's missus had suggested. An ancient water-cooler sent a pleasant breeze in her direction. There were wet patches beneath her armpits, and another halfway down her back. Perhaps she could plan things out better with her eyes shut.

When she stopped going to school, she and Sua often sat in the big bed and coloured in all afternoon. They used the seventy-two colour pencil set that had been Amanda's seventh birthday present. They had modern art books and Buddhist mandala books, and a good collection of tattoo-design books, all made for colouring. Amanda liked to keep the pencils in the original order, and carefully sharpened. Sua taught her how to crosshatch, how to blend. Whole afternoons passed this way, two bent figures gently shading between the lines.

'Imagine you all alone in strange house.'

Sua had whispered this story, as if the walls themselves might eavesdrop.

'The man who keeps you there – The Fiancé – sometimes he takes you out, but always close. You are like a dog on a lead. The house he keeps you in has a high fence. All the windows have metal screens, dark glass. You dream about escape, plan all the time. But you have no money, no passport. The man, he threatens you. He says he will kill you if you try anything. He allows one thing. He lets you post a letter home sometimes.

'One night The Fiancé takes you out to dinner at a big hotel with some of his clients. When he gets a drink at the bar, his friend asks you if you are happy in his country. "No," you say. "I want to go home." "So, why don't you go?" the man says, and just then The Fiancé comes back and takes your elbow, and he moves your body away from the other man, so you cannot talk. But you remember the stranger, he has a smile in his eye, a kind heart. After that, you listen out for his name when The Fiancé speaks on his mobile phone. You look up his number when The Fiancé takes his shower.

'One day, The Fiancé goes out to work and does not come back. Three days. Three nights. He does not come back. You work at the window screen with a knife, you turn the screw. When you make it outside, you are not sure. What can you do? You walk in a garden. You go along the street. Then you walk a long way to a shopping centre. You get a taxi. You take it a long way. You go to the kind man's house.'

After hearing this story, Amanda found herself thinking about The Fiancé. She worried he might come for them. Sometimes she felt she could actually hear his approach. There he was in the creaking tin roof. Or there, in the scratching branch against the window. Sometimes he lay so quiet in the shadowlands beneath the big queen bed, she could swear he had stopped breathing altogether.

She turned about in the little iron bed in the farmer's spare room. She could hear movement in the kitchen, and the low murmur of voices, as the adults sat down to their late Sunday lunch. Water was dripping somewhere. Plop, plop, plop. The cooler. Just before Amanda drifted off, there was the fleeting image of the old man, bent over his walking stick, treading carefully on the orange pebbles along the slope of a bush firebreak. Perhaps he was catching up to her, in his own time.

CHAPTER TEN
KITCHEN WORK

It was half after two when Dave again made his way through Movement Control. Screws lined either side of the gateway, arms crossed, legs slightly apart, a mix of solemn pomp and casual disinterest. Dave placed one foot in front of the other, a kind of mechanical doll. It seemed to him he had been walking inside exactly this kind of wire and steel enclosure, concrete underfoot, for most of the years of his life, uniformed figures, like angels of menace, sternly monitoring his progress. Even on the outside, some larger presence had always seemed to keep him corralled, making him small, standing between him and all the things that might otherwise have been possible. Dave Loos was a body, walking a preordained line.

There was a time, when he was a kid, when he had believed in God. Nan Halliday used to take him to St Matthews, the old Anglican church in Armadale. Father Allen. Father Brian. Decent blokes, he supposed now, though at the time they seemed unusually effeminate men. Perhaps all deeply religious men were like that. There was something slightly unreal about them, as if they'd never been sullied by the kind of violence Dave and boys like him faced everyday in the schoolyard. Nan had him confirmed. There was no question of whether he believed in God: he did. But it was a childish faith, a task of the imagination. He had perhaps believed in God the way other children believed in fairies or gnomes.

Was there a point in his life when he stopped believing? Nan Halliday died. He hadn't been to church since. Maybe it was one of those things: you hang out with believers, you start to believe; you hang out with nonbelievers, well ... it seemed to Dave there were few believers left. No one in the can had faith in anything much, not governments, not churches, not schools or universities, certainly not the law. And how could you separate God from his institutions? The faith from the church?

Corporal Steven, whom he met later, at the drop-in centre in the city, had spent more time with the adolescent Dave than anyone else. He was a Salvos bloke, a believer, but rougher around the edges than those Anglican priests of Dave's early childhood. They're a blur now, those years Dave spent on the street, more like hollowed-out time. Hours sitting slumped in sheltered alleys down from Perth station. The itchiness, constant itchiness, the aggression. And Corporal Steven, giving him a second chance, a third chance, more. The guy was a fool, or else ... what?

Dave cut vegetables. He cut them every weekday afternoon, facing a stainless steel table, one of four. The other blokes, one beside him, one in front, one diagonally opposite, cut the same vegetables at the same time. It sometimes felt like working before a three-sided mirror. Even the sound of the knives buffing against the chopping boards threatened to synchronise. They were almost always the same kind of vegetables. Mostly it was potatoes, carrots, pumpkins. Sometimes broccoli, cabbage, beans. Four pairs of hands sliced and diced and stewarded the pieces into white plastic containers, one for each unit.

Bear usually made the kitchen work tolerable. A Maori fella from Rotorua, a huge clown with a round Buddha's face, he goofed off to the riff of long-forgotten eighties soundtracks, or else flirted with the vegetables: 'How is it for you, bitch?' Bear helped the others through the afternoon with long, involved stories about ugly women he'd fucked, or comic tales of break-and-enters gone wrong. But if you weren't in the mood, he could be agonising. There was no excuse for a long face, where Bear was concerned.

Dave put on his apron, took up his knife, nodded to the rest of them. He felt kind of morose. There was no hiding it.

'At low tide ants eat fish, at high tide fish eat ants,' Sua had said to him once. Some Thai proverb. He was thinking of it now, supposed it was the same as tables, and how they turn.

His mind shifted back to the night he opened his

front door to find Sua standing on the front doorstep.

'Please, can I come in?'

It was half past ten on a weeknight. The kids had come down with a gastro virus only twenty-four hours earlier, both of them sleeping listlessly in their shared room, their temperatures high. Dave was exhausted. He had already cancelled his shift at work for the following day. His body ached.

Sua's presence on his doorstep disturbed him. He remembered her, of course, and wondered about Manning, but something about the way she stood there suggested she had put the other man behind her. The lights of the taxi that had delivered her to him were already sailing down the long driveway to the quiet road. She had marooned herself.

There was little need for words. She followed him inside. Their bodies brushed against each other. Her hand found his. Dave knew nothing of Manning's fate as they made love on the lounge room floor. Nothing had prepared him for the overwhelming experience of making love with Sua. Before this sex had been urgent and mechanical – and mixed, afterwards, with a queer sense of shame. Was it because they were complete strangers to each other? Or was it because they knew each other long ago, as Sua sometimes argued, lifetimes ago?

When he woke up in the night, her face was inches from his own and she was watching him. She blinked. They could hear one of the children calling out to him from further down the hall.

'Dad?'

Dave swallowed and looked closely at Sua's face.

'What do you want from me?' he whispered.

Sua closed her eyes and said nothing.

Bear was doing his *Good Morning, Vietnam* thing. He could recite the whole of the opening sequence. He was good at it. He had the whole Robin Williams DJ persona down pat. Then the songs: The Beach Boys; Frankie Avalon; Wilson Pickett; The Searchers. Sometimes they went back to Bear's room after the shift, shared a can of drink, played a few cards. Put on the *GMV* soundtrack. Not today.

Sometimes you spend years looking at things the wrong way, Dave thought. You assume that what you're looking at is a bunch of tulips in an elaborate vase. Then somebody draws your attention to a shape in relief and you pull focus and see instead a vivid pornographic illustration. And it had been like that all along, everybody knew, only you were looking at it the wrong way and you felt foolish for ever having imagined anything fancy or beautiful.

Dave felt outside himself, somehow, distant. He watched his hands chopping vegetables. Beneath the table, his right foot tapped nervously. The prison kitchen felt vaguely like a stage set. Only he wasn't sure what was going to play out there.

As a con, you learned to live with regret. There was that day during the winter, for example, when Sua booked her first and only visit to the prison, and he shied away from seeing her. It was a cold, wet day and she came without the girl, during school hours. Probably, she would have had to get the Transperth bus all the way in to Midland, then backtrack up the hill on the prison service, sitting there with all the welfare mums, her small frame sinking into the big seat, the other women and their kids all loud and ballsy and crude. He pictured Sua looking quietly out the window of the bus, then waiting in the visitors hall, all those people hugging and smiling and then himself, a brutal coward, stalling at the entrance to the building at the last minute, the other cons brushing past him. Did she sit there for the full hour? Or did the screws shuffle her out when it was clear he'd lost his bravado? How ill was she, that day, he wondered. Did she already have the diagnosis? As it turned out, it had been his final opportunity to lay his eyes upon her. And he'd refused it.

He scraped cubes of potatoes into a white plastic container. There was some kind of soundtrack to it, some kind of rhythm too, the knives.

It wasn't until after that visit he discovered Sua was seriously ill. It was Amanda who told him. Poor kid. She didn't even know what AIDS was. Dave knew Sua had been in the sex trade. He knew the whole story. Her uncle came to get her from school one day when she was thirteen. He told her he needed her to do a favour for a friend of his. 'It's very important,' he said, 'that you do whatever my friend asks of you. It's a matter of honour.'

She spent three years in the service of her uncle's friend. He owned a brothel in the Muslim south.

Dave felt so angry, thinking about what had happened to her. She was only a child. When Sua first told him, he wanted to chase that brothel owner down and string him up by the balls. Sua tried to console him.

'Something very small keep me going all those years,' she said. 'It was a little shape.' She pressed a thumb into her palm. 'The shape was like a leaf.'

She described the washroom in the old family shophouse in Ubon where her mother kept a tall container full of water; the family washed with a scoop from the big tub. It was a simple room, with a squat toilet and the tub of water and no taps. Her mother scrubbed it every day. Often the neighbours were coming and going from the house and shop. There was no need for invitation, upstairs or downstairs, no need for knocking. People came and went from one another's houses as they pleased. The only place for privacy was the washroom. But it was so full of mosquitoes that you didn't want to linger.

The floor was tiled, as were the walls, up to about two-thirds of the way to the ceiling. What Sua treasured was an imprint, trapped like a fossil in the stuccoed wall, three-quarters of the way up. It was the shape of a leaf. It had been there for as long as she could remember. It was there when she was so small that her mother did the washing of her body for her. Sometimes she shut herself in that dank little room just to look at it. When she was locked up in her uncle's friend's house, she thought of that imprint, of how the leaf itself, the one that made the impression, must have turned to soil years ago, but something enduring was still left of it. Something beautiful had survived. When she returned home to her province so many years later, she found strangers inhabiting the old family home, and was directed to an outlying village, her paternal grandmother's village. Before she left the old house, she requested to use the washroom. The newcomers had retiled the walls, but only up as far as the old line of tiles. Above that, the leaf's imprint remained, even beneath a fresh coat of paint.

'This is it for me, darlin',' Dave remembered telling Sua once. 'I mean it. I want to grow old with you. I want nobody else.'

They would have married except for the visa situation. It would have meant her having to leave the country, and perhaps a ban on her re-entering. They didn't want to take the risk.

By some cruel miracle, Dave was HIV-negative. The health staff had tested for all sorts of shit when he came back to prison. He had ongoing issues with hep C, and the staff deemed him a candidate for 'at-risk behaviour'. They noted a history of addiction and a term in Graylands Hospital in his late teens suffering from what was then known as amphetamine psychosis. They noted a diagnosis of adjustment disorder during a stint in Canning Vale more than a decade ago. When the counsellor questioned him he reported suicide ideation, but he agreed that it was only fleeting, because of his kids. He had no plan to carry it out, he said.

'We can put you on Largactil,' said the medic.

'No,' he said. 'I don't want it.'

He didn't want to join the ranks of Lofty, every day a half-deadened dream.

He sliced carrots, round and bright, a perfect circle at the core, and thought of Sua's father. It occurred to him that this morning's no-show was deliberate. It was the old man's way of making his judgement on Dave clear. The son-in-law was a jailbird, a con, a useless piece of shit. The old man had every right to ignore him. Sua was gone. And Dave had walked out on her. Not just her. He'd walked out on his own kids.

CHAPTER ELEVEN
A FATHER'S EMBRACE

Amanda raised the window in the farmer's spare room and pushed her face against the flywire, taking in the warm air. The wire smelled of dust. Two sheepdogs were sleeping in their baskets on the long verandah. She could hear one of them mock-barking in its sleep. The rest of the house was still. Outside the afternoon sun continued its quiet project, baking the stubbly paddocks to a charred gold. Nothing was moving.

She crept out into the hallway. The passage to the kitchen and dining area was closed off. Amanda opened the heavy front door without the slightest squeak and retrieved her shoes from among the others on the verandah. Behind her, the two dogs stirred and whined, then just as quickly, settled. She was soon following the farmer's potholed driveway all the way down to where it met the Great Eastern Highway. As she reached the road she felt satisfied with her decision to leave the house. Across the way was the Doconing Road T-intersection.

It was the back route to Chidlow her dad always used to take after a few beers out at El Caballo. For the first time since early that morning, she knew precisely where she was.

Interstate trucks made their way along the Great Eastern Highway with a great roar of noise and movement. Sometimes a passenger car slowed, its brakelights flickering, as if deciding whether to slow and stop. Mostly they were going too fast to manage it anyway. She didn't want them to, her heart beating fast whenever one threatened to do so. She was grateful when they disappeared from view.

As she walked, she made a mental list. It was a game she played whenever she felt the need for hope. She took one good thing from everyone she knew and aspired to be a new person made up out of all the good bits. She decided she wanted to be like her dad for all the things he knew about the bush. And she wanted to be like Ant for his duck's back – Dad said the weight of the world rolled off Ant whereas Amanda took things too much to heart. She wanted to be like her teacher Mrs Sweeney for the confidence she carried in her hands as she sketched animals in chalk. And the school gardener, Bill, the most practical of people she had ever met. Where was he? What would he say to her now, if he knew the mess she'd got herself into with losing the old man? If she could be like Sua, she thought, if she could just have Sua's courage, nothing would ever frighten her again.

She wondered again about Sua's dog Juum. She still

felt bad about what she had done. Things turned strange the day Sua died. In the late morning, after Ant came home and the ambulance officers arrived, Amanda sat outside and watched strange lights appear in the treetops, pretty white splinters, shifting like ice shards in moving water. She was dazzled by those lights, even as she sensed that they were not really there. Speaking was difficult, too. Which is why, when she had tried to speak reassuringly to the dog, all of her phrases were full of corners and spikes. Nothing worked. Juum cowered a few feet away from her, spooked as much by the queerness of her voice, as by the presence of strangers in the house.

The dog had turned up on the doorstep one weekend, filthy and totally underweight. Sua took him in. He had always been a sorry-looking thing. He was always shivering, and when he wasn't shivering he was just standing around, reluctant to move, even when you fell right over the top of him.

In hindsight, the dog must have known that Sua was dead well before Amanda discovered the fact. He had spent the night shuffling up and down the hallway while she listened to the tap-tap-tap of his overlong nails on the bare wooden floorboards and drifted in and out of sleep. He wandered about like this sometimes when it was stormy, but that night had been clear and still. Yet he wandered and whimpered until Amanda, too, lay awake, tired, and a little bit frightened. Ant was out, as always, just out, and Sua had been too weak to speak or sit up for nearly three days.

The last time they had talked, Sua told her about a dream she'd had about Dad. They were down at the zoo, the whole family, and Dave was holding Sua's hand. They were looking at the old enclosures where the zookeepers used to keep the animals in the olden days. The cages were fashioned like caves, small and cramped, with thick black bars on the front. Dad started goofing around, pretending to be trapped in one. Then a fruit bat flew out of the dark, skimming the top of his head. He ducked with fright, and everyone laughed.

'That's a pretty ordinary dream,' Amanda had said.

'They're the best kind,' said Sua. 'They are the ones that sometimes come true.'

That morning, the ambos had been full of questions. They asked and asked, and Ant had grown angry with Amanda's constant mumbling and her dull repetitions: I dunno. Ant was always nervous with people in uniforms. But what did they expect her to say? They were asking her things she didn't have answers for. Besides, everyone knew it didn't matter now. Sua had been dead, they said, for at least twelve hours. The officers, a man and a woman, were a long time at the house. They said that because there had been a death they had to call in Forensics. When the other car finally arrived, it turned out to be a kind of a police car, with blue and white checkers on the side. The men wore coveralls. That's when the white-tailed black cockies arrived in the big trees, screeching. That's when Amanda decided to do what she did with the dog.

She was pretty sure Ant didn't know about Dad's

bunker. She was pretty sure nobody knew. It was built beneath the concrete floor of the old rainwater tank up in the back corner of the block. It had a door like a safe, with a keypad lock, disguised by a row of coffee rocks and some old steel rubbish that blended in with the rest of the junk around there. Dad had taken her there three different times, the last time early one morning during the Christmas holidays. The space inside the bunker was dark and damp, and just big enough for two people to sit down, but there was a fluorescent tube hooked up to a twelve volt battery, so you could switch some light on, and that's how she'd first seen Dad's treasures. He had money in an old wooden fruit crate, quite a bit of money, all notes. That last time, he showed her the new things: an antique Buddha rupa mounted in glass, and a steel tube full of white powder, portioned carefully into clip-lock bags.

'Mum's the word,' he'd said to her, and winked. 'I just want you to know what's here, sweetheart, in case anything should ever happen to me. Don't come too much. Actually, you shouldn't come here at all, unless it's really necessary. I don't want you wearing a path to the door.'

When the men in coveralls entered the house, Amanda picked up the dog and hid behind the new garage. The dog would not bark. It never did. Juum was only ever capable of whimpering. The two of them, scruffy and panicky, sneaked from tree to tree and up to the rainwater tank. Ant would have to deal with the men on his own.

Now it was clear the big birds gathering in the old marri were going to be there for a while. There was a great racket. They were Carnabys, as big as cats, and ten times louder. Hooligans. They threw honky nuts onto the roof of the rainwater tank and laughed. The smaller birds, the family of finches that Sua had always kept watered near the house, flitted in and out of the scrub, following the progress Amanda and the dog made towards the tank, almost fussing over them, as if they were babies.

Once she and Juum were inside the bunker with the door closed, they could barely hear the birds. It was cool and dark. The dog's tongue was warm and rough in the palm of her hand, and they could both take comfort in the faintest scent of Dad, though it had been months since he'd been there.

Six years, the judge had given her father. She would be fourteen before he got out. What was she to do without him for so long? And now without Sua as well? The dog was shivering again. She would stay here, she decided. She would stay here with the dog until everyone in the house had gone away.

A ute slowed on the highway just ahead of her. The left blinker went on as the vehicle shifted to the verge. It was some distance ahead, but she could see the silhouette of the lone driver through the rear window. She stopped walking. At that moment, the road was mysteriously devoid of other traffic. Amanda's heart quickened. She could almost hear her own pulse thud-thud-thudding in her ears as she went scrambling into the roadside gully. This part of the road was newly surfaced, the edges laced with fresh blue metal that was unstable underfoot. Amanda slipped, damaged a knee, then crawled, stood up, ran. She had no idea where she was heading. The nearby bush was scraggly, uneven, no place to hide. 'You just follow your feet,' her dad had told her once, when they went creature-spotting in the reserve one night and their torchlights died. 'You just follow your feet.' The line repeated in her mind, the memory of her father's voice a shadowy comfort. Somewhere in the distance, a car door slammed. Then a road train passed above her on the highway: *whoosh*. Just as quickly, gone.

A little way ahead, the gully was met with a series of huge stormwater pipes running beneath the road. She kept her head low, and felt her way towards the mouth of one of the pipes. The sun beat down on her back. When she reached the entrance to the first pipe, an ominous shape spooked her, and her heart jumped. It turned out, on closer inspection, to be a sheet of black plastic, flapping. She crawled in, squatted down and settled, pulling the black plastic across like a scrim. She could hear voices, speaking in low tones. So there were two people?

She kept still. It would not last long. They would be gone soon.

Her legs had been aching for some time, and it felt surprisingly good to sit down, especially away from the heat of the sun. The pipe had that damp-sand smell about it. After a while she detected a soft dripping noise.

It was coming from further inside the tunnel, where the light fell to darkness. She blocked out the echo of traffic above, the sound of the distant voices, footsteps on blue metal. She focused instead on a softer sound. Drip, drip, drip. It was a kind of music. Drip. It was the same gentle rhythm that had sent her off to sleep in the farmer's spare room.

Amanda leaned back against the curve of the pipe and imagined her father beside her, a heavy arm across her chest, the smell of Port Royal tobacco. He had a way of nestling her on the lounge in front of the TV at home, so that she could lean her cheek against his shoulder and watch the light from the screen washing his face one colour then the next. He had put her to sleep like that since she was a baby. She had lost count of the number of times. Once, at the prison, they were told off because she sat too long on his lap. She thought she saw tears sparkling in her dad's eyes once the guard moved on, satisfied. Sometimes they needed each other close, she and her dad.

She still remembered the first night after the court case, so many months ago now. Amanda had moped around the house, drinking hot Milo, playing with the cat. Sua and Ant were sitting out on the verandah, drinking coolers.

'He's an idiot,' said Ant when Amanda came out to graze a hip against Sua's chair for the umpteenth time. The phrase had stayed with her. Their father was an idiot because he had held up a bank alone in broad daylight, no escape plan, no weapon. 'Like he was just saying, "Come and get me, ya cunts," ' Ant reckoned.

At school, after the sentencing, the teachers gave Amanda sympathetic looks. She tried not to acknowledge them. She was not the only kid at the school with a parent in jail, but in her heart she felt unique enough.

Her Dad wrote her letters.

Dear Bub

Here's one for the collection:

Q. When is a car not a car?

A. When it turns into a garage.

Love you to bits.

Dad.

That was what they'd always said to each other: love you to bits.

The floor of the concrete pipe was hard against the bones of her bum. Her knee was bleeding. She cupped a hand over the wound, then scraped the blood with her index finger, and put it in her mouth. It tasted sweet, slightly salty. Her thoughts fell, once more, to Juum. He shouldn't have started to bark, that's all. Why did he decide to give them away like that? He'd never barked in his life. It felt like betrayal. She kicked him until the bark turned to a whimper and then she kept on kicking. She kicked him until his fur came loose in clumps against her boots. She kicked him until he stopped moving. And then the sound of voices erupted outside the door to the hideaway and she was ashamed, deeply ashamed. She cuddled up to the dog then, burying her face in his little shoulder, both of them stone quiet.

Even now, her toes ached from that kicking.

CHAPTER TWELVE
THE HOLD-UP

Rattuwat had already been walking for a long time, across one ridge, down another. At home in the rural north-east there was no way you could walk for so long and not come across a group of workers, a hut, the edge of a village, someone to invite you to drink and eat with them. Why hadn't the man in the distant tractor noticed him, he wondered? Was he a walking ghost? It sometimes seemed that he had been walking in a kind of geographical loop, traversing the same patch over and again, the variation in his surrounds so limited.

Sometimes he called out the girl's name.

'Ananda! Ananda!'

But the only reply was the receding thump of kangaroos or the empty harking of a crow.

He followed what he imagined to be the girl's continued path, the original paddock long having fallen away behind him. But he was conscious that he was, by necessity, making things up as he went along. He carried with him nothing but a set of car keys and a shabby wallet in his back pocket, along with a few loose coins that clinked about in his shirt pocket. There was a thick milky stickiness inside his mouth, the product of thirst.

The old man was grateful that the pain in his chest had abated, but his tread was, as ever, careful. He travelled down another shallow gully and up the tender slope of the other side. As he reached the ridge, the grey line of the highway came into view, a kind of scar, and he imagined he could hear, just faintly, the distant rumble of a long-distance truck. This mark of civilisation frightened him after so many hours of emptiness. Its appearance was brash, surprising. Had the girl come as far as the road? A new concern for her welfare awoke in him. The thought of her stumbling through paddock or scrub was somehow less disturbing than this threadbare highway along the sides of which no pedestrians ambled. He made for the road's edge, climbing carefully between the wire fencing separating one paddock from the next, and when his sandalled feet crunched against the gravel along the verge of the sealed road, he looked east, and saw the great figure of the oncoming long-distance truck. It passed him in a rush.

Once at the road, he did not know the direction to take. He did not know north from south. He turned right. Whether he was heading towards the broken-down car, or the elusive prison, he was not sure. Under the circumstances, either would do.

Some time later, a gradual bend in the road opened out to reveal a small shophouse surrounded by a sprawling gravel carpark. There was a truck pulled up at one end of the vast expanse. Rattuwat made his way gradually towards the white-brick shopfront, his mouth watering at the thought of a cold drink. His flip-flops picked up tiny gravel missiles as he went, shooting needle-like pain up the back of his legs.

In the solid shade provided by the shopfront, Rattuwat rested a short time beside a display of motor oil. He was catching his breath. From where he stood he could see the petrol station attendant serving an Aussie in a blue singlet. The customer looked unhappy. The shop attendant's gestures seemed to indicate an attempt at polite placation. Rattuwat understood well the finer arts of this particular situation, and his thoughts rested with the shop attendant. As he waited for the discussion to conclude, he fingered the hem of his back trouser pocket. He retrieved his wallet, and it took him a moment to identify and separate the five dollar note from the ten. An electronic doorbell sounded as the other customer exited the shop, swearing beneath his breath.

As Rattuwat entered the building, the blast of cool air hit him with dramatic force. It was like entering a new world. The light was cool and white. The floor was smooth and hard. He made his way to the brightly lit refrigerator, gazing at endless rows of cool drinks in all manner of colours and containers. He helped himself to a familiar red and black can and carried it across to the shop attendant.

The young man was dark-skinned, perhaps Indian or Sri Lankan, and impeccably well groomed. 'Two eighty, sir,' he said. Rattuwat sensed the attendant's skills were wasted in such a backstop, dealing with the likes of the man in the blue singlet. He could be working in a high-class hotel in the city. He was probably a university student, Rattuwat summised, working his weekends in an ordinary job to help to pay his way through his degree. 'Two eighty, thank you,' the young man prompted again. He spoke with an English far more musical than the mumbled monotone of the farang children who had been living in his daughter's house.

Rattuwat passed him the five dollar note, then looked about for somewhere to sit. It was not polite to stand and drink, but the can in his hand was beckoning, its cool exterior already wet with condensation against his warm palm. His head began to ache.

He sat, with some degree of difficulty, on one of several tall stools overlooking the carpark. He drank quickly, almost dizzied by the sweet cool touch of liquid in his throat.

The young man behind the counter also stared out the window at the near empty carpark. The two entered into an easy silence.

'You are walking?' said the shop attendant, after a time.

'Yes, yes. The car stop and then it not start.'

'Whereabouts?'

'Same road,' said Rattuwat, gesturing, then wondering if indeed it was the same road. 'I think same, this one, yes.'

The young man nodded, waiting for him to say more.

'Sorry,' Rattuwat said, his head aching more fiercely

now that he had sat down, 'I not sure. I not sure where am I. The car no good, then we start to walk. The girl say she know where to go.'

'The girl?'

'The girl,' Rattuwat confirmed, unsure how far he should trust the stranger. But the young man was so earnest. 'She a Western girl,' he elaborated. 'You see her?'

'I have seen plenty of Western girls,' the attendant laughed. 'You will need to give me some more detail.'

Another customer pulled up. Rattuwat and the attendant watched as the man filled his tank, then stepped into the store to pay. He gave the attendant a plastic card, pressed some buttons on the console, then left again, having barely grunted at either of them.

'My granddaughter,' Rattuwat said, his voice trailing off in thought.

The other man chose not to respond.

'A prison near here, yes or no?' he asked.

'Yes, a few kilometres away. Acacia Prison,' the attendant confirmed.

'The girl's father in the prison.'

'Actually, there are two prisons nearby.'

'Two?'

'Two. One is a prison farm.'

'The girl know the one.'

'What did he do?'

It seemed almost too personal a question.

'Not sure,' Rattuwat answered honestly.

'One prison is low security – the prison farm. The other one, Acacia, it's for medium security. So, it depends on the nature of the crime.'

'I am old man. I cannot walk long way. But the granddaughter, I hope she go there.'

'Where did you last see her?'

'Many hours. Not sure. She say she walk to prison.'

'Is there someone you can phone?'

'Could phone. Yes.'

There was Tui, the daughter of one of his work colleagues in Bangkok. She had married an Australian and was reportedly living in Perth, but Rattuwat had tried phoning her that first day he arrived. The number had been disconnected. It had not occurred to him to write down the mobile phone number of the girl's brother, Ant. He had only the phone number of the son-in-law's house, and he suspected that nobody was home there.

'Do you have a mobile?'

'No.'

The two returned to their companionable silence. Rattuwat could hear the soft murmur of a television jingle, the screen evidently hidden somewhere beneath the counter, for the young man kept staring down there. The headache was making its presence felt via an unrelenting thumping at Rattuwat's temples. Perhaps he was dehydrated. He had already drained the can of soft drink, but his thirst felt barely quenched. He sat for a time, then reluctantly recounted his change. He should not spend it, he thought, but his stomach was singing for food and he had soon slipped off his stool, and was making his way back towards the refrigerators.

There, he examined rows and rows of soft drinks. The Roman script was mostly unfamiliar to him, though some of the brands were the same as he got at home and he recognised several logos. He chose a garish orange can, then shuffled along one of the aisles until he recognised a self-serve hot-dog vendor. He used tongs to retrieve a red sausage from the vat and placed it on a warm, white bun, squirting the lot with bright red sauce and mustard from a couple of large plastic canisters. This was the kind of thing they sold at the 7-Eleven near Park Plaza Sukhumvit, back at home, three times the price of the street vendors, and not even half as good as Thai food. Thawin would be shocked to see him eating it. Never mind, it would do for now. At the counter, he paid out the change from the five dollar note to the shop assistant, but was forced to retrieve the wallet again. The ten dollar note was soon exchanged for a few small coins.

Rattuwat felt a victim to his own foolishness, but lacked the inclination to reverse his actions.

There was something about the stool overlooking the long carpark that suited him. He spent some time watching the trucks moving along the highway or pulling in and out of the roadhouse for fuel. A few customers came and went. Perhaps this was as good a place as any to wait, he thought. If the family were to come looking for him, they would see him here, even from the carpark.

Time passed.

He asked the boy about the bathroom, and was

directed through a swinging door at the back corner of the shop and down a narrow hallway piled with boxes, where he pissed miserably into a stinking trough. The washroom tiles were in need of a good scrub, and somebody had graffitied something unreadable across the mirror above the sink. As he made his way back along the hall, he heard a vehicle screech noisily to a halt in front of the shophouse. Youths were shouting at one another over the top of a car stereo, which boomed and thumped aggressively in a style familiar to Rattuwat from Bangkok. It was clear to him as he moved quietly along the back hall, even without fully comprehending what the voices were saying, someone was here to cause trouble.

Rattuwat's whole body began to tingle. He felt a sudden, desperate urge to get outside, to breathe fresh air: the corridor was too narrow, the light too sallow.

'Fuck off, Jordie!'

'Ant, get some smokes, mate!'

'Dumpy, take the safety off.'

The clarity of these voices was almost surreal in the dim hall. He recognised something in one of them. He wanted to call out, but could no longer find his voice. He stepped forward and lost his balance. As he fell, he was loosely conscious of a pile of boxes coming down with him.

Then, out of blackness, Rattuwat took the form of a warm glow that floated along the stained back hallway of The Lakes Roadhouse, gliding towards and beyond the swinging doors that led out to the shop. Here, he took in the stiff body language of the shop attendant, the false bravado of the three would-be thieves, just children, brandishing metal bars. He travelled out of the building and saw the battered car, the baby-faced fellow behind the wheel, chewing his fingernails. He saw into this boy's heart. He loved him.

When he returned to himself the floor tiles gave a firm, cold comfort. It took him a few moments to remember where he was. There was a dull pain at the back of his head. He wiggled his fingers. There didn't seem to be any blood. With some effort, he turned onto his side and eased himself up to sit. There was a squealing noise, which he gradually registered as the sound of car tyres, and then the bubbling of a big exhaust as a vehicle accelerated into the distance.

The first thing he saw as he stumbled back into the shop was the face of the shopkeeper, a great toothy smile, beaming.

'Thank you, Uncle, thank you.'

'What happen?'

'That big noise you made back there. You scared them off!'

Rattuwat nodded in recognition. He had seen nothing, but at the same time, he knew: the voice of the ringleader belonged to Dave Loos' son.

'Uncle, you don't look so good. What happened back there? Are you okay?'

CHAPTER THIRTEEN
CLOSER TO GOD

Dave's feet led him from wall to wall, forward and back and forward and back. In the pause, right there, as he turned and blinked, he remembered Sua holding Steve Manning's hand, as he'd seen them do that first day at the courthouse. Steve Manning bought houses for cash. He took advantage of punters down on their luck. He paid twenty-five per cent below market price. He owned ten or fifteen places at any one time. He could store goods for you, short-term. That's how Dave and John came to know him. That's how he came to be called to witness in Harley Trembath's court case. But that image of Sua and Steve Manning holding hands as they shuffled into the foyer of the Central Law Courts, it revisited him often. Sometimes it gave the impression of two people deeply in love. The supportive woman, accompanying her partner to court. But on other occasions it seemed the man was guarding the woman, keeping her close, pressing his palm just a little too firmly against hers.

Elsewhere in M Unit, the fellas had come back from the footy, a hint of drunkenness to their banter, though none had access to spirits. It was glory that intoxicated them; their team had won. Dave knew he should make his way down to them, to sit and smoke and jibe the late afternoon away, they could help his mood to lift. But the legs jittered, the teeth were pushed hard to the jaw, and he knew his presence would only bring his mates down.

He breathed out.

On a good day, in Acacia, Dave was nobody. He had no family to speak of, no life beyond the gleaming steel perimeter. To be nobody, to have no expectations, it was a trick only occasionally sustained. Today, he had not been able to convince himself it was so. The day's events had roused the ghosts of all his disappointments.

Lofty hovered at the door to their cell, his drug haze evident in his silhouette, a kind of travelling cloud. Dave felt as close to Lofty at that moment as a brother, as if they had known each other their whole life. And yet he could no more be confined to the cell with him than he could reverse the events that led to Sua's death.

He got up, brushed past Lofty, and approached the smoking figures of the other M Unit cons in their post-footy huddle. A few heads turned towards him only to register a kind of dull recognition. Dave had no intention of squatting beside them. What he needed was height. He hoisted himself up onto the big wheelie bin near the external door and stretched a hand up towards the guttering of the roof. He was David Sebastian Loos, just as they had announced him in court that first time, decades ago. He was David Sebastian Loos, the product of all his errors, yes, but also a good father, for the most part, a good man. The sudden firmness of his knowledge gave him a sense of conviction.

If you pushed the door to the unit back firm against the brickwork, you could use the horizontal bars just like a ladder. Up he went, but not without exertion. The guttering cut into his fingers. A knee bashed against the corner of the door. Beneath him, some of the fellas were getting up from the concrete, extending their limbs, looking up.

'What's up, bro?'

'What you doin'?'

What Dave wanted was the gift of air and light. What he wanted was to be closer to God.

'Don't be an idiot.'

With a quick shifting of his weight, then a sharp breath in, he was up on the roof.

The late November sun was glaring, almost painful.

As he stood tall, he felt a sting at the base of his spine, burning. Had he been shot? The pain seared, and for a moment that was all he could concentrate on, just that beautiful rush of heat, white, pure. After a few moments, he opened his eyes, and he was conscious of the wire fence, his fingers entwined in it, the way he was lifted, somehow, by the steel paling. He looked up and saw a crow flying through the air above him and he wanted to cry out to it.

'Caaw,' he tried, but his voice wouldn't come. 'Caaw.'

If the bird could get a message to Sua somehow, he could tell her about that soft velvet cloth in the little trunk beneath the rainwater tank, all the cash he had wrapped in there, the jewellery he'd set aside for her, and something else, that amulet she gave him, it was wrapped in the velvet. It was all there in the bunker, Amanda knew where.

Then something shifted. He was on the roof, flooded with light, bending forward, unsteady.

He remembered taking Sua to the zoo, early on, to meet Bill and Pam. It was years ago now. 'We barely know each other,' he'd confided to Bill. The women walked a little behind, speaking quickly in their musical language. 'Just enjoy yourself, Dave,' Bill reckoned. Sua had been at Dave's place precisely one week. The kids ran amok; there were crocodiles and brightly coloured parrots and a new baby giraffe to look at. Pam pushed her newborn son in the pram while the girls looped back and forth and back and forth, relaying an excited garble of information about the next attraction.

Dave felt suspicious of Sua, even then. But at the same time it felt good to have her walking beside him, paying him attention. Was it an act? When a bird landed on her shoulder she had it climb onto her finger and passed it across to Dave. It made him laugh, and he remembered the way she had pressed her mouth against his the night before, and he shut his eyes a moment and wondered, for the briefest time, what it might be like to have a girl like her with you all the time.

When they rounded the corner near the duck pond to stop for lunch, he realised that she had looped her arm inside his and that they had been walking along like that for some time. He couldn't remember the point at which it happened, only that they were walking close and he was smiling, and it felt like a beautiful day, and when he looked at Sua the sun shone off her dark eyes. The kids could see what was going on quite clearly, and so could Bill and Pam, and nobody minded, and everybody was happy, and it felt right.

Another two weeks would go by before their first full night alone together. They left the kids with Adie and his missus overnight and Dave took Sua to a seafood restaurant in Northbridge. They sat across the table, looking at each other. He took in her exquisite, carefully made-up face and felt he didn't deserve a woman like her. Her calf grazed his and he took hold of her wrist and smiled at her, despite himself.

After the meal, he looked her in the eye and said, 'I give up.'

'What do you give up?'

'Everything.'

At home, they made love until they were sore, and still he couldn't get enough. The next day, before they picked up the kids they drove down to the beach near Hillarys and they sat in the sand and she leaned back against his embrace while they looked out to sea. When she turned to face him he traced a finger down from her forehead, across her nose, lingered at the edge of her mouth.

'You're so beautiful,' he said.

She closed her eyes and held her face close to his and bit his ear and then she said, 'I love you, Dave Loos. I loved the first time I saw you.'

'No, you don't.'

'I do,' she said, laughing, but he swallowed and pushed her away.

On the way back, in the car, he went all nervous again. He had never felt so overcome in his life.

Sua sat beside him and said nothing. When they pulled into Adie's driveway he held her arm, tight, before she could get out of the door.

'Sua, I'm begging you,' he said. 'If this is a set-up, you have to say.'

Her face went stony.

'Please. I need to know. Who? When?'

'Believe me,' she said. 'I don't know what you are asking.'

He never got the full story. He still wondered, even now, about Manning. What does it mean to kill? The cons he'd known who'd got done for murder wore it like a badge. But it had to feel different from the inside. He had never gone so far himself, couldn't imagine it. In the haze of grief after Sua's death it sometimes didn't seem to matter so much, the part she had played. He didn't know what Manning had done to her to make her feel the way she did. He only thought: she loved that man once. Jealousy coursed through him. And then he remembered the electrical wire, and he knew he could not love a woman who could do that to someone who'd slept, night after night, close beside her. Steve Manning left for work on his motorcycle one morning at the usual time. At the corner of Jones and Hargrave, one block from home, someone had tied a tightrope of electrical wire just at the right height to catch a motorcyclist by the neck.

According to police reports, a motorist taking the same route only seven minutes earlier reported nothing suspicious. Someone had timed it perfectly for Steve Manning's passage.

Dave was standing at the roof's apex now, only distantly aware of a familiar noise echoing below him. It was the prison alarm system. He watched the swift movement of screws, like toy soldiers, across the quadrangle below. One of the medics was cupping his hands, looking up, squinting.

He had never experienced anything quite like the panic and disorientation he felt when he discovered that reel of electrical wire almost a year ago. It was hard to find words for it. What came between him and Sua was an otherwise ordinary coil of blue insulated wire, coded for neutral, and unearthed beneath the floorboards of their bedroom by chance. Dave found it amongst her most precious things: a necklace, all the letters written to her from her folks. And in his heart he knew. He thought: *There, but for the grace of God, go I*. She had set Manning up, and never breathed a word of it to anyone. Further, the guy had that many links to organised crime, everybody blamed somebody else. Sua knew it. Now

Dave knew it. He feared the depth of her callousness.

Everything he'd done since then, he could see now, he'd done out of fear.

So, he put himself back in the can. He put himself back in because it's what he'd always done. People expected it of him. And she couldn't touch him in here.

He could only vaguely remember walking into the bank in Hay Street that weekday morning, last summer. His heart was black. The only medicine he knew was obliteration. He thought: if Sua were ever to fall in love with someone else, she would betray me as quickly as she betrayed Manning. He threatened the teller with a blunt weapon, nodded at the cash till. Didn't even need to speak.

And now, beneath him, Code Red. The prison had gone into lockdown.

The heat of the steel roof numbed his skin. And yet, the skittish feeling that had been building in his body back on the ground was starting to evaporate up here. The new vantage point reminded him of the jacaranda tree in the park down from his mother's house in Armadale, back when he was at primary school. He and his mate Luke used to spend hours up there. Once, when they were about Amanda's age, they stayed up in the tree all night, drifting in and out of sleep, draping themselves across the sturdiest high branches. They watched all the Friday night drunks wandering home from the pubs, and discovered that if they kept quiet enough, people rarely looked up. Luke pissed on some poor drunk. The guy looked up, and still didn't register.

Not so here at Acacia.

They were putting a ladder up, lining up the dogs.

'I'm here for my kids,' he might say to the screws. No, he didn't know what he would say. He was a dumb cunt who'd let his kids down already. He no longer felt capable of speech.

The last of the afternoon sky was the deepest, clearest of blues. He wondered about the colour of the atmosphere. What was it that gave emptiness colour? He remembered being fascinated by the same question as a teenager. The answer was something to do with the atmosphere being dense close to the earth's crust. Something to do with the colour blue having the shortest wavelength. He hadn't understood it properly then. He didn't understand it now. But it was nice.

A flock of birds were vying for a drink at a leaky sprinkler over by the north fence. Smart bastards, those crows. How he hated their cawing, the sleek black polish on them, their relentless, menacing presence.

He could hear someone speaking to him from the edge of the roof. The words flowed over him, but he felt unwilling to decipher their meaning.

He watched as a lone galah landed on the sprinkler top. A fool of a bird, but at the same time plucky, a cheeky bugger. The galah marched at the crows, took over their ground, shoved his beak to the water with such a sense of ownership that the crows waddled away. Then another galah arrived, and another, until the whole flock descended, twenty of them, thirty. A great, gaggling raucous bunch. You had to smile at them.

You had to admire their class.

'Dave?'

Four fingers pressed against the rim of the guttering. He could see the nails going white with pressure.

'Mate,' said a familiar voice, 'come down now, buddy, before the shit really hits the fan.'

The sky was blue because of Rayleigh scattering, he recalled. It was nothing to do with God.

'Dave, come on, bro. Get down, before they throw you into DU.'

No one could tell the precise point at which atmosphere became space, solidity became air.

I'm not here, he thought, and was quietly satisfied with the idea. I'm not here.

They would come and force him down soon enough. He knew it. They would throw the bloody pharmacy at him, drug him up like Lofty, or worse. The two of them would make a fine bloody pair, delirious, half-dead.

Harmless, but; harmless, eh? That was the main thing.

CHAPTER FOURTEEN
THE EDGE OF THE ROAD

'Let me call you a taxi,' Darjuna offered, having found the old man a more comfortable chair. 'Where are you staying?'

'Mount Helena.'

'Where?'

'Mount Helena.'

'Where's that?'

Rattuwat passed the slip of paper he had been carrying with him in his pocket, on it the address of his son-in-law's house.

'Oh, Mount Helena,' Darjuna confirmed. 'It is maybe fifteen minutes' drive. You want a taxi?'

'How much?'

'I don't know. Maybe fifteen, twenty dollars. I don't know.'

'Too much. You can do. I give you five dollars.'

'I'm not a taxi driver.'

'No, but you can do, yes? I give you five dollars. Can?'

'You want me to drive you?'

'After, after. When you finish job?'

'Not till seven thirty.'

'Okay, good. You drive me. Seven thirty. Five dollars.'

'Uncle, you have to wait another two hours. Maybe longer. I need to put in a police report about those kids.'

'Okay. I wait.'

'All right. And, you know what? You don't have to pay me, Uncle. I'll do it for free.'

Amanda could just make out a slumped grey carcass up at the edge of the bush. At first the figure looked almost human, but as she got closer, its features sharpened. She slowed her pace, then stopped. The animal had been hit by a car. It was not yet dead, and lying on its side. When it sensed her, it raised its head, twitched its ears. A big grey roo. Amanda's presence set the animal straight into the heat of panic. Its whole body twitched and shook, then shifted into the dumb shudder of a full-blown fit. She caught in its eye that distant, fearful gaze, the same one she had witnessed in the eyes of Sua's dog.

What she wanted to do was help. She stepped a little closer. The beast twitched and arced and then, as the fit subsided, lay still, only the chest expanding, collapsing with exhaustion. It seemed kind of absent and yet at the same time she knew it was completely aware of her. Amanda tried to keep still, breathe easy, to transfer a sense of quiet comfort, but it didn't seem to make any difference. Now what? Her feet were heavy, as if rooted to the earth. She could not move. A car rushed past them.

Whoosh.

Amanda fingered the small Buddha rupa she had kept in the pocket of her dress since the day of the kicking. She found herself thinking about Juum, how he kept so close to her lately, as if to remind her of what she had done. He had a permanent limp now, and yet he seemed to love her the best since Sua had gone.

The roo rested its head on its chin, then swallowed. Amanda was conscious of her own breath, in and out, in and out. She watched the animal's dark wet eyes glisten. They were alike, both stranded, in their own way.

Amanda could almost hear the roo breathing.

When the second fit began it went on and on, so that the shuddering became all there was to the world. It echoed Amanda's shifting pulse. Shutting her eyes, blocking her ears, nothing helped. But she could not move away. She stood and stood.

The day was winding down, the heat sagging. A fly crawled along one arm, then nestled in the corner of her eye. She shooed it away. It returned. She shooed it again. There was the distant cawing of crows. No movement. No traffic.

When Amanda looked once more at the furry body at her feet it was clear that the roo was dead. She squatted beside it and placed the palm of her hand on its still warm shoulder. Then she walked on. She did not want to see the crows descend.

Darjuna's car was only operating on three cylinders. It backfired twice as they made their way along the highway, every other vehicle roaring past them at speed. They were looking directly into the sun, which was finally lowering in the western sky. Darjuna squinted. Rattuwat felt at ease beside him.

'Your father must be happy. You a good boy,' he said, and when his observation was met only with a polite nod, he wondered whether he had made the same comment already. Indeed, the phrase had a familiar lilt to it. The young fellow was embarrassed, perhaps.

'Actually, my father died in an industrial accident, when I was a child.'

'Oh, sorry.'

'It's okay. It is just a fact. Fortunately, my mother has a good education. Now she runs a small women's refuge in Kandy,' he said. 'It is the only one of its kind in my province. She is doing good work, but it is not easy for her. Sometimes she is threatened personally. I hope that when I finish my studies, I will be given permanent residency in Australia. Then I can send for my mother, and my brothers.'

'How many brothers?'

'Six.'

Rattuwat nodded, more to himself than the boy. He was thinking, once more, of his daughter's letters home. He hoped that Darjuna's situation was different, would go on being different.

Up ahead, the lopsided carcass of a hotted-up black sedan became visible at the road's edge. One of the back wheels was missing. Amanda recognised it as Ant's car, but was also acutely aware that there was something different about it. Someone – a stranger – had been tampering with it in the hours since she and the old man had left. The thought unsettled her.

And yet, as she touched the warm paintwork, a sense of belonging arose. She opened the unlocked back passenger door and climbed in, as if coming home. Inside, the air was thick and hot. She wound the windows down then sank onto her back against the warm seat. She closed her eyes. Her skin was damp with sweat; a trickle ran down into her ear. Her mouth was clammy, swollen with thirst, but for a time all she could do was slump there. Then it occurred to her to look in the boot for water. Dad used to keep a full container there in case the radiator overheated. When she finally raised herself up and got out, she smiled to see the same old plastic juice container. Two litres of water. She drank it gladly, even though it was hot and tasted of dust and petrol. She drank and drank, then wiped white stuff and little bits of blood away from her lips. Afterwards, she lay down on the seat again and the heat didn't matter because she was almost asleep. She was having that dream again, the one about the turtle. Maybe she had always been the turtle, old, old, older than the old man Rattuwat. She swam between shards of light that beamed down from the surface of the water and it was like a kind of dance, this swimming. She was Amanda Jane Loos, all turtle, and she was living beneath the surface, vaguely conscious of having to wait for Dad or Rattuwat or Ant, but she could have spent whole lifetimes happily in that state, because she knew one of them would come.

Later, the sun had fallen so low that the landscape was tinted with colour. She stood, part leaned, loosely between doorframe and car body, staring into the nearby paddock, and singing a little song: Here I am, here I am, here I am. She tapped her fingers to the rhythm on the roof of the car. She did this for a long time.

Sua was ghastly to look at towards the end. Amanda covered the mirror opposite the big bed with a sarong, but Sua pulled it down. One night the two of them sat wakeful in the darkened room, holding hands. 'Beauty falls away,' Sua told her. 'Pain, too.' Amanda didn't reply. Her palm was all clammy and hot. 'When you let go of pain,' she whispered, 'there is only love. This is all we have.'

Her brother's half-stripped car was suddenly too small for Amanda. She slammed the door, and walked away, leaving the fluffy dice swinging. Anger propelled her now. She was angry with Ant, angry with her father, angry with the old man. She was angry with the doctors and angry with the police and angry with the bland, pitiful kindness shown to her by the farmer's wife. The girl did not know where she was going. That much was true. But she was going there anyway. She was going there with bells on. She was travelling with Sua in her heart.

They rounded a bend and Rattuwat recognised the vehicle immediately.

'Stop. Stop. Darjuna, here! My son-in-law car.'

His heart was beating fast. No sooner had Darjuna pulled to a stop and Rattuwat was out of the vehicle.

'Ananda?'

Darjuna was close behind him.

'Is she there?'

The vehicle was like a long-forgotten toy, rediscovered. The black and white dice swung in a ridiculous fashion, like something from a cartoon. Rattuwat never thought he'd be so happy to see them again. The car's bonnet was flung open, just as they'd left it that morning, a gaping mouth. A wheel was missing.

There was nobody there.

Afterward, as the two men drove on, a silence grew. Rattuwat's companion seemed to understand something that hadn't been spoken between them. The road stretched out, empty of life. Then, as they rounded another bend a road train passed – *whoosh* – and revealed in its wake a small movement, a fleck of red at the roadside.

'Do you see that?' Darjuna asked.

The old man couldn't, at least not at first. Everything was blurry. Then, as he squinted, he could just make out the shape of a girl. She was walking, unaccompanied, into the glowing dusk.

NOTES AND ACKNOWLEDGEMENTS

This novel was initially inspired by The Jātaka, stories of the Buddha's former births, that date back to at least 380BC. There are some five hundred and fifty separate fables that go to make up the collection broadly known by contemporary readers as The Jātaka. I began the novel with a selection of these and set about recasting them into a single narrative and a contemporary Australian context. In interpreting the original Jātaka stories I have relied heavily on the six-volume collection translated from the Pali by various hands under the editorship of Professor E.B. Cowell and published by Munshiram Manoharlal Publishers Pvt. Ltd in 1990 (my own edition reprinted in 2002).

As my own work progressed, I became less concerned with keeping true to the original Jātaka, and more concerned with crafting a sense of unity for the narrative as a work of fiction. Those who are familiar with the Pali Buddhist canon may recognise the traces of some of the original Jātaka tales, and those who are not will, I trust, enjoy a different but no lesser reading of this novel on its own terms.

I am also indebted to the following works for reference and inspiration: *Childhood* by Leo Tolstoy; *Many Lives* by M.R. Kukrit Pramoj; *Memoirs from the Women's Prison* by Nawal el Sa'adawi and *Very Thai: Everyday Popular Culture* by Philip Cornwel-Smith.

I am grateful to the following people and organisations for assistance, encouragement and advice during the writing of this story: Warwick Bell, Ron Blaber, Liz Byrski, Nadine Davidoff, Maureen Gibbons, Brendan Hebbard, Cheryl Kershaw, Natalie Kon-Yu, Steve Mickler, Georgia Richter, Rachel Robertson, Neville Sweeney, Lyn Tranter, Sister Ajahn Vayama (Dhammasara Nuns' Monastery), Yvette Walker, Curtin University, Western Australian Department of Culture and the Arts, the Literature Board of the Australia Council, and all the staff at Fremantle Press. Thank you also to the staff at Curtin University Early Childhood Education Centre for the excellent childcare services that made the completion of this work possible.

Twenty-five percent of author royalties from the sale of this book will be donated to Australia for UNHCR. Australia for UNHCR is an Australian charity that aims to help Australians to change the lives of refugees and displaced people around the world:

http://www.unrefugees.org.au

First published 2013 by
FREMANTLE PRESS
25 Quarry Street, Fremantle 6160
(PO Box 158, North Fremantle 6159)
Western Australia
www.fremantlepress.com.au

Also available as an ebook.

Consultant editor Georgia Richter
Cover design Ally Crimp
Cover image iStockphoto: Corridor of Prison with Cells
Printed by Everbest Printing Company, China

National Library of Australia Cataloguing-in-Publication entry

van Loon, Julienne
Harmless / Julienne van Loon
1st ed.
9781922089045 (pbk)

A823.4

Government of **Western Australia**
Department of **Culture and the Arts** | lotterywest | Australian Government | Australia Council for the Arts

Publication of this title was assisted by the Commonwealth Government
through the Australia Council, its arts funding and advisory body.